CHAPTER ONE

Ewww," Inessa Weaver cried, wrinkling her nose. "Look at that awful looking man over by the side of the road!"

Jaris Spain was driving his younger sister, fourteen-year-old Chelsea, and her friend, Inessa, to the mall. They were going to buy new summer outfits. It was late on a summer afternoon. The kids were just out on summer break, and the first day of school seemed far, far away. Both Chelsea and Inessa would be freshmen this year at Harriet Tubman High School. Jaris was going to be a senior.

"He's got something in his arms," Chelsea pointed. "It's furry looking, and it's moving and,"—Chelsea shuddered—"it looks all bloody and stuff."

"His face looks so weird," Inessa commented. "He looks like one of those guys in horror movies."

Jaris slowed down his car and began pulling toward the curb near the man.

"You're not going to stop are you?" Inessa screamed. "That monster could attack us!" Only the seat belt was keeping Inessa from scrunching down onto the car floor.

"Oh, Inessa," Chelsea scolded. "Don't freak. That's just some poor guy who had an accident or something. It's not his fault he got burned in a fire or something."

"Probably got hurt in the war," Jaris remarked. Once the car was stopped, Jaris could see the bloody creature in the man's arm was an opossum. "Hey bro!" Jaris called out to the man, who looked about thirty-five or forty. "Opossum get whacked by a car?"

The man nodded. He had one good eye. The other eye was covered by a patch.

Inessa covered her eyes with her hands and crouched in the car. She couldn't stand to look. "I get them all the time," the man answered. "Wounded opossum. Cars hit 'em. Sometimes big dogs tear 'em up. Poor little critters. They're trying to make their way in a world without much use for them. They're like the rest of us, I guess."

Chelsea looked out the window of the car. "What's gonna happen to the opossum you got there?" she asked.

"I'm part of an opossum rescue group," the man explained. "We bring 'em back to health, or we put them down painlessly. Not right to just let them die in the street or the brush. Too much suffering there."

Chelsea stepped from the car. "Can I see it closer?" she asked. Jaris got out too.

"Chelsea!" Inessa screamed. "Don't go near that man and that horrible animal."

"I'm Jaris Spain," Jaris said, extending his hand. "This is my sister, Chelsea. We're Tubman High students. Chelsea loves animals."

The man took Jaris's offered hand with his left hand. That hand wasn't bloody. "Hello," he replied, "I'm Shadrach." He had once been handsome, but something had happened to his face. His right eye was gone, and the right side of his face was scarred. He was tall, about six feet, and he had a nice smile. Chelsea liked him immediately.

Shadrach looked at Chelsea. "Would you like to learn more about the opossum rescue work?" he asked her. "If so, go to Shadrach.com."

"Do you help the opossums all by yourself?" Chelsea inquired.

"No, people help me, people like you. Check out our Web site," Shadrach responded.

Chelsea looked closely at the beady-eyed little opossum with the pink nose. "Good luck, Mister Shadrach," she wished, meaning the opossum and the man.

When Chelsea got back into the car, she spoke to Inessa. "You shoulda come with me and seen the opossum, Inessa," she said.

"It was so cute. And the man wasn't bad either. He's just hurt. He rescues wounded opossum. That's really nice, I think."

"They give me the creeps," Inessa complained. She was relaxing a little now that the car was moving away from the man and the opossum. "Sometimes at night the opossum come in our yard, and I'm afraid to go out. They're so spooky. My pa goes out and chases them."

"I saw a TV piece last month," Jaris remarked. "It was about the work the opossum rescue people do. It's pretty cool. They even got a nursery for the baby opossums. They say sometimes the mother gets killed, and the babies are still alive in her body. Sometimes they can save the babies."

"Maybe I could do something like that this summer," Chelsea thought. "I could volunteer at that place."

"Yeah, chili pepper," Jaris agreed. "That'd be good."

Jaris thought volunteering like that would keep his little sister out of trouble.

While she was an eighth grader at Marian Anderson Middle School, Chelsea had a few bad scrapes. She started hanging with a creepy Tubman freshman, Brandon Yates. He lured her to a party, where the kids were drinking liquor, and doing drugs. Jaris had to rescue her.

Then she went for a wild ride with Yates and his dopehead brother Cory. They'd pulled up in front of Marian Anderson Middle School in a silver Mercedes. The boys talked Chelsea, Athena, and Keisha into taking a short ride with them in the car. The ride turned into a dangerous high-speed race on and off the freeway. Luckily, no one was killed.

After that, Pop came down hard on her. He grounded her for a long time. In fact, Chelsea was still grounded. She couldn't go anywhere by herself. Normally, she and Inessa would have taken the bus to the mall by themselves. But Chelsea was grounded, and her freedom was curtailed. Jaris felt he was the one who was suffering for her mistakes. Either her parents or Jaris had to drive her. Mom kept promising that maybe she'd get her freedom back when she started as a freshman. But she'd have to convince her father first that she was responsible.

On their way to the mall, Jaris drove past Spain's Auto Care. Pop, Lorenzo Spain, had just bought the garage where he had worked for many years for old man Jackson. The Spains had to put a mortgage on their home to buy the garage. But having the business meant the world to Pop. Mom had to swallow her fears of having a big mortgage so that Pop could have his dream. Jaris's parents fought for weeks over risking everything for the business. He and Chelsea listened fearfully while their parents argued.

"But what if you fail, Lorenzo?" Mom had wailed.

"What if you trusted your husband more, babe," Pop had answered.

Now, as Jaris passed the garage, he slowed down and hit the horn. Pop was working on an old Chevy Malibu. He turned, grinned, and waved.

"Pop's smiling a lot more these days, huh, chili pepper?" Jaris commented.

"Yeah!" Chelsea agreed. "He used to be so gloomy all the time. He kept saying he was just an old grease monkey. Now he owns his own business. I'm so happy for Pop."

The girls peered silently out the car windows as Jaris thought about how things used to be. He remembered the many times his father came home from work, angry and frustrated. He was always talking about his bitter regrets. A sports injury had kept him from his dream of winning an athletic scholarship to college. He felt like a loser most of the time. Sometimes Pop was often down and depressed. A darkness seemed to engulf the whole house. Even Jaris felt overshadowed by it, and he thought maybe he was a loser too.

"I'm gonna text Athena," Chelsea declared. "She said she might meet us at the mall. That'd be so fun. Athena is fun to shop with."

"I don't want *her* shopping with us," Inessa grumbled. "She's always getting into trouble."

Chelsea had to admit it. Athena did have a way of attracting trouble, but she was Chelsea's best friend. Inessa was nice, but she was too cautious. You could hardly have any fun with Inessa.

"Athena's okay, Inessa," Chelsea responded, texting her.

"My parents don't want me texting and tweeting and stuff like that," Inessa commented. "My father says that's all a big waste of time and money. My dad works hard, and he can't afford nonsense."

Meanwhile, Chelsea got a text back from Athena. "She says she can't come," Chelsea reported. "I'm gonna ask her about her rescuing opossums this summer. Would you like to do that too, Jaris?"

Jaris smiled. "I'd like to chili pepper," he replied. "But this summer I'm gonna be working almost full-time at the Chicken Shack. I gotta save money for college. And I'd like a better car. I'm driving one of those beaters Pop is always talking about."

After a few minutes, Chelsea groaned, "You know what Athena texted me? 'ROTFL.'"

Inessa stared at Chelsea, "Why did she say that?" she demanded.

"She's rolling on the floor laughing," Chelsea explained grimly, "because she doesn't want to work with the opossums. But I sure do. I mean, I've always thought maybe I'd be a veterinarian or something. Working with animals appeals to me. That'd be a good way to find out if I'm good at working with animals."

"Well, check out Shadrach.com, Chelsea. See what he offers," Jaris suggested.

Chelsea rolled her eyes. "Like Pop's gonna let me go and help Shadrach with the opossums!"

"I sure wouldn't let anybody I cared about go near that horrible looking man,"

Inessa announced. "He looks like the monsters in those scary movies. You gotta be careful of people like that."

"Inessa," Jaris explained, "in the movies the bad guys are made up to look scary. In real life, some of the worst crimes are committed by handsome dudes. I don't know about Shadrach. We'd have to know more about him. But he could a wonderful man, maybe a war hero. And if that's so, we oughta be honoring him for his sacrifice instead of being scared of him."

"He couldn't be a war hero," Inessa insisted. "I bet he's a crook who was trying to burn down a building. He probably got hurt that way."

Jaris shook his head.

A minute later, the Honda pulled into the parking structure at the mall. "Now, lissen up, girls," Jaris commanded. "Buy some nice stuff and get it done. I'm not spending the whole day sitting on a bench while you guys try on everything in the stores."

"You could buy stuff too, Jaris," Chelsea suggested. "You always wear those old jeans and T-shirts."

"I hate shopping," Jaris responded. "I love my old jeans and shirts. I hate spending money too." Jaris was like his father in that way. Pop wore stuff until it fell apart. "Do you see Pop hanging around the stores? Does he go feeling the fabrics and turning the stuff around and around like you guys do? That's a girl thing."

They all got out of the car and started toward the mall entrance.

Jaris was like his father in many ways. He had the same deep insecurities that plagued Pop. Next term, Jaris wanted to enroll in Advanced Placement American History. The course was taught by his favorite teacher at Tubman, Ms. Torie McDowell. But he wasn't sure he was smart enough to get college credit while still in high school. He thought he could do the work, but maybe not. There would be awfully bright kids in that class. Jaris worried whether he might be over his head. Yet he wanted those college credits, and he'd feel like a coward if he ducked the class.

Jaris and the two girls walked down the wide promenade with stores on either side. Loud rock and rap music poured from the Tiger's Paw, a popular teen apparel store. A look of excitement lit up Chelsea's face. "Oh Inessa!" she cried, grabbing her friend's arm. "Athena got an amazing top in here last week!"

"They sell really skimpy stuff," Inessa noted.

Jaris groaned. The last thing he wanted to do was go into Tiger's Paw and rub shoulders with an army of hysterical thirteen- and fourteen-year-old girls. An elderly man was sitting on a bench outside the store. Jaris had planned to buy a tall, iced coffee and join. But he knew what would happen if Chelsea brought home more short skirts and skimpy tops. Pop would go ballistic again. He would roar around the house like a wounded lion. He'd rant that his little girl was "goin' wild again." Mom would insist Chelsea was just dressing like her peers, and his parents would be at it again.

Jaris walked into the store with the two girls. The only other boy in the place was a kid about fifteen with a magenta mohawk. His arms were covered with tattoos, mostly of skulls. Jaris tried to pull his head into the collar of his T-shirt, like a turtle pulls in its head. But he couldn't do it. Jaris spotted some fairly modest, brightly colored T-shirts. He pointed and suggested, "There! Look at those great T-shirts. They're on sale too."

"I hate them," Chelsea declared. "They're so last year." She elbowed two twelve-year-olds out of her way to get closer to a rack offering scoop-necked tops. "Inessa, look!" she screamed. "This is what Athena got." The boy with the magenta mohawk looked startled, and he moved out of Chelsea's way. He thought something terrible may have happened, as if the clothes might be diseased. Jaris thought that any-thing was possible in this dark, spooky place that smelled of incense. Jaris smiled weakly at the magenta mohawk. He ex-plained, "Just excited little girls, man." He felt an unlikely kinship with the boy.

"This is it!" Chelsea screamed again, clutching a lilac-colored scoop-necked top. Jaris was getting what Mom would call a "splitting headache."

"Get it in a large enough size, chili pep-per," Jaris sighed. "So you're not, you know, falling out of it."

"I take really small," Chelsea insisted.

Jaris was almost knocked off his feet by two hefty fifteen-year-old girls. They were dashing to the jeans counter. A trembling pink light indicated that prices had just been slashed. When he recovered his bal-ance, Jaris gritted his teeth. He commanded Chelsea, "Take a medium and a small, and try them on. *Now*."

Chelsea emerged from the fitting room, spilling out of her small top. Jaris had a nightmarish vision of Pop seeing her in this top headed for school. In his mind, he could hear Pop bellowing. "All the punks gonna be droolin', little girl. Oh yeah. They gonna be droolin' so much they're gonna need to change their shirts. Y'hear what I'm sayin'?" Jaris couldn't face it. Since Pop had coerced Mom into signing the new mortgage, the feeling around the house was miserable. Jaris didn't want to risk a fresh war over Chelsea's risqué clothing.

"Chelsea," Jaris declared grimly. "Go back and get the medium one for cryin' out loud!"

"Jaris!" Chelsea wailed. "Inessa, tell him the truth! Isn't this just perfect on me?"

"If *I* wore something like that," Inessa replied, "my father'd make me wear a pullover. And I'm not even built like you, girl."

"Thank you, Inessa," Jaris said.

"You're a traitor, Inessa," Chelsea screeched.

"Get the medium one," Jaris advised through gritted teeth. "*Now*."

Chelsea wanted to protest further. But she saw the growing rage in her brother's eyes and decided arguing wouldn't work. She returned to the fitting room, tried on the medium top, and came out saying, "It fits like a tent, but I'll take it."

"Now get the jeans," Jaris commanded.

"I'm a size two," Chelsea announced at the jeans rack.

Inessa laughed. "Girl," she snickered, "you can't fit into size two jeans. You'd look like pork sausage in those casings!"

"Size six," Jaris snapped to the young male clerk. Jaris thought to himself, "Dude how do you stand working in here?"

In about an hour and a half, Chelsea bought two tops and a pair of jeans. Inessa bought a workout wear. Jaris herded the girls toward the parking structure with their bags. He looked at his watch. He had enough time to drop off the girls and get to work at the Chicken Shack. After work, he wanted to pick up Sereeta, his girlfriend, and get some frozen peach yogurt at the Ice House.

As they drove for home, Chelsea texted Athena. She said she had two cute new tops, but they were miles too big for her. It was all Jaris's fault because he was even worse than Pop. In the seat next to Jaris, Chelsea mumbled what she was texting Athena.

Jaris tried to get Chelsea's mind off the size of her new clothes. "Be sure and try Shadrach.com, chili pepper," he urged her. "Sure would be great if you spent the summer working with the opossums."

He thought, "Better them than me! If Chelsea gets busy with the opossum population, there would be fewer trips to the mall and other places."

CHAPTER TWO

Jaris was going to drop Chelsea at home, then Inessa at her house.

When they got home, Mom was there. "Well," Monica Spain asked, "did you guys have a nice shopping trip?"

"Marvelous," Jaris responded dryly. "Couldn't have been more enjoyable if I'd had a root canal at the dentist's."

"Oh, Jaris!" Mom laughed. "You're getting sarcastic, just like your father. Sometimes I think you're turning into a carbon copy of him."

Mom's smile faded. "I would hate for that to happen."

"Jaris spoiled everything by making me buy clothes way too big for me," Chelsea complained.

"Well," Mom explained, "you know how your father gets when you wear tight clothes, Chelsea. We don't want to upset your father anymore than he already is. He's trying to run a business along with being a mechanic too. He's bitten off way more than he can chew. All he needs now is to see you strutting around in tight jeans and a top showing off too much of your . . . figure."

"I don't strut, Mom," Chelsea whined bitterly. "I mean, I'm not some trashy—"

"Now's the time to check out the opossum deal, chili pepper," Jaris suggested.

"What opossum deal?" Mom asked. "What are you talking about? Why am I the last one to know anything around here?"

Inessa piped up. "Oh, there's some totally gross man who takes care of dying opossums in a shack or something. I mean, he only has one eye, and he's all scarred and stuff. Chelsea wants to go there and be his lab assistant."

"*What?*" Mom gasped.

"No!" Jaris almost shouted. "He's a nice guy who takes care of hurt and sick opossum. His name is Shadrach, and he's seems to have a heart of gold. He's probably a wounded veteran, and we're gonna check him out on his Web site."

"He was all covered with blood when we saw him," Inessa commented. "I got sick."

Jaris took a deep breath. "The opossum was hurt, see," he explained. "Cars hit them, and they lay injured, just suffering. This guy picks them up and takes them to the opossum refuge center. It's not just him. He has lotsa volunteers."

"Ewww," Inessa wailed. "It was the most disgusting sight I've ever seen."

"Sometimes I hate you, Inessa Weaver," Chelsea scolded. "Sometimes I just hate you. If you weren't my friend, I'd smack you in the face right now."

Chelsea went to her room with Inessa and Jaris to check Shadrach out on the computer. Mom hovered over them, a frightened look on her face.

Chelsea brought up Shadrach.com and there was a nice picture of Shadrach. "Look!" Chelsea cried triumphantly. "He doesn't look bad at all. He looks nice."

"It doesn't show his bad side," Inessa insisted, scowling.

"There's a picture of the little place where they work with opossum," Chelsea went on. "It looks nice. Inessa! Look, there's a teacher from Tubman. She's in charge of getting volunteers from her science class to go work with Shadrach. Students get credit and everything. We'll probably be in her class."

"Well, I'm still afraid of him," Inessa said.

"There's a picture of some Tubman students!" Chelsea cried out. "Oh, I wanna go right over there now."

"Tonight?" Inessa responded. "To the monster's laboratory at night?"

"I gotta get to work," Jaris groaned. "Mom, can you drop Inessa home?"

"Sure, honey," Mom agreed. "I can do that."

"And then we can go to Shadrach's place, huh Mom?" Chelsea asked.

Mom's eyes grew wide. "It'll be pretty late after we drop Inessa home," Mom noted. "Maybe we could do that another day, huh, sweetheart?"

"That man is so awful looking," Inessa remarked. "He's got just one eye."

Chelsea gave Inessa a poke. "You already said that, dummy! Mom, please? It'll be a couple hours before Pop gets home. I *know* he'd take me, but I don't want to bother him when he's working so hard. It's just over on Indigo Street."

"That's in a real bad neighborhood," Inessa commented.

"No, it's not!" Chelsea insisted. "Mom, we could drop Inessa home and then just go over there real quick. You could meet Shadrach, and I know you'll like him."

"I suppose so," Mom relented. She had a look on her face as if she'd just bitten into a lemon.

After they dropped Inessa home, Chelsea started chattering. "Mom, maybe I'll wanna be a veterinarian when I grow up. This would be a cool way to find out if I like working with animals. I mean, they raise babies and heal wounded opossums. I'd just get a taste of everything. Opossums are marsupials, you know."

"Yes, I know," Mom replied. Even as a child, Mom never wanted to have anything to do with wild creatures. The house cat was as far as she wanted to go with animals. She wasn't even too crazy about the cat. "I uh . . . was never into wild things, sweetheart," Mom confided. "I mean, I enjoyed watching nature movies and all. But I never wanted to get up close with *them*."

"Oh, I love animals," Chelsea chirped. "You could tell that Shadrach does too. He was so nice and kind with that hurt opossum. He didn't even mind that it was bleeding all over him."

Mom's lips tightened, and she blinked her eyes a couple of times. Chelsea regretted her words. "I mean, just bleeding a little," she corrected herself. "But Shadrach was so gentle."

"Well, sweetie," Mom suggested, "don't get your hopes up too high about working at the rescue place. This man may be very experienced with this sort of thing. He might not want a girl your age working there, you know." Mrs. Spain looked hopeful. She was praying that this strange, frightening man might say, "Thanks, but no thanks." Then they could get home before darkness fell.

"Mom," Chelsea noted, "it says on the Web site that Shadrach works with a lot of middle schoolers and high school kids. Oh, Indigo Street's coming up."

Disappointment clouded Mom's face. "Well, he might prefer boys. Girls don't like the messy stuff around animals."

"Oh, that wouldn't be fair," Chelsea declared indignantly. "Girls can do anything boys can do and maybe do it better."

Mom smiled over at her daughter. "Things get so dirty and awful around animals, and you're such a dainty little girl," the mother remarked.

"No, I'm not," Chelsea protested. "I'm not prissy like Inessa. I'm tough. I don't faint and stuff when I see blood. Like when the family dog poops at Inessa's house, she's like grossed out, but I don't care."

Indigo Street was not well kept up. At best, some of the homeowners struggled to keep a little green in their front yards. For the most part, the yards were dirt, littered with old tires, sofa pillows, kids' toys, even some mattresses.

At the end of the street was a frame building with cages and runs in the yard. Mrs. Spain recognized the place. Some years ago, it had been a small veterinary clinic. It had gone out of business. People didn't have the money to pay for their pets' medical care. Two large pepper trees softened the appearance of the place and provided shade.

"This must be the place," Mom noted, pulling into a pitted driveway. "Needs resurfacing, huh?"

"It said on Shadrach's Web site that they need donations. I guess most people don't care about opossums," Chelsea remarked.

Mom had a look on her face that Chelsea could clearly read. "I, too, don't care about opossums," Mom was thinking. "In my book, my dear, they are the same as rats. If all the opossums of the earth vanished at the stroke of midnight tonight, it would not bother me. True, I'm sitting in this crumbling driveway in front of this ratty old house. It's getting dark, and the place gets scarier by the minute. I'm here only because I love you, Chelsea dearest. I want to help you fulfill your newest hare-brained scheme of becoming a rescuer of opossums."

Chelsea hurried toward the peeling front door of the house. Mom followed, looking around nervously.

After they rapped several times, the door opened. Chelsea had already seen the severely scarred man, so she wasn't shocked. Mom was clearly upset. Chelsea knew Mom had a big heart, and she reached out to a lot of poor and unfortunate people. But she was unnerved by someone as damaged as Shadrach. Maybe after a while she'd get used to him. But right now she looked as if she wanted to be anywhere else on earth instead of here.

"Hi, Shadrach," Chelsea hailed. "Remember me? Me and my brother talked to you today when you were rescuing that opossum the car hit. I went on your Web site, and it was really interesting. I thought maybe I'd like to be a volunteer or something."

"Okay," Shadrach responded, "come on in." He glanced at Chelsea's mother. He knew the look on her face. He saw it a hundred or more times on the faces of people meeting him for the first time. "Oh my," they'd think, "what happened to that poor man?" Their eyes would quickly be downcast. They didn't want to stare.

Shadrach smiled. Smiling always helped a little.

"I'm Chelsea Spain and this is my mom, Monica Spain," Chelsea made the introductions. Shadrach made no effort to shake hands. Some people didn't want to shake hands with him. Some might even think he looked as he did because of some terrible disease. When Jaris Spain reached out today to so readily take his hand, Shadrach was touched and surprised.

"Well, Mrs. Spain and Chelsea, have a look around," Shadrach suggested.

Opossums were everywhere. Some were scrambling around in cages. Some, obviously hurt, lay still. Chelsea peered into one cage. "They're cute," she remarked. "This guy seems to be sizing me up. Look Mom. Look at how he stares at me with those bright little eyes."

"How wonderful," Mom replied. She looked very unhappy. She folded her arms tightly around herself. She seemed to want to be smaller and less likely to touch anything around her.

Shadrach reached into the cage and gently lifted out the opossum that had been looking at Chelsea. "This is Magic," he explained. "He's doing really well. I'm getting ready to turn him loose pretty soon. You shoulda seen him when we found him. He was stuck in a pipe. He ran in there to escape from a big, mean dog. Then he was stuck there for days, no food, no water."

Shadrach held the creature at arm's length and looked at his face. "Poor little guy. He was scratched and bruised when we finally got him out. He was near dead. But he'll be good as new pretty soon. Want to hold him, Chelsea?"

Mom shrank back, shielding Chelsea. "But they bite, don't they? I mean, it's a wild animal. I don't want my daughter getting bitten. I imagine they even have rabies," Mom cried.

"Yeah, sometimes they'll bite," Shadrach admitted. "But Magic won't. And you can't get rabies from an opossum. Their body temperatures are too low for the rabies virus to take hold in them."

Chelsea reached out and took Magic from Shadrach's arms. "Oh, I'm not afraid of you, Magic." Shiny black eyes, like polished buttons, peered up at her.

"You can't get anything from an opossum that hurts people," Shadrach explained. He smiled a little. "He likes you, Chelsea. He tolerates most people, but he likes you."

Then he looked at Chelsea's Mom and continued. "I've worked with raccoons, and you can get rabies and parasites from them. Raccoons are a lot more trouble than opossum, but they have their place in the world too."

Shadrach took Magic from Chelsea and put him back into his cage. "Won't be long now, buddy," he told the animal. "Freedom!"

"You should see them when we let them go," Shadrach said. "It's pure joy. I love these little creatures. They value freedom as much as people do, maybe more sometimes."

"Well, this is all very interesting," Mom remarked, looking at her watch. "So do you want to think about this, Chelsea, and come back another time?"

"Maybe you'd like to see the babies before you go," Shadrach suggested.

Chelsea's face lit up. "Oh yes!" she cried.

Shadrach led them over to a large plastic container. He lifted off the top. The tub was filled with newspapers and food. In one corner of the tub was a fleece bag that, to the babies, felt like a mother opossum's womb. Shadrach reached into the bag and gently pulled out a tiny creature with big eyes and ears. It chirped like a cricket.

"Oh my," Chelsea gasped. "It doesn't look like hardly anything. Where do you get such little ones?"

"The mother opossum was killed," Shadrach answered. "She lay on the road with her babies alive in the pouch. A lady saw them and called me. I went out there and brought them in. It's pretty tricky taking care of the tiny ones. You gotta thread little tubes down their necks to feed them. You have to do it just right or you'll hurt them."

"You have to know what you're doing around here, I guess," Mom commented. Her message to Chelsea was clear. Mom didn't say it out loud, but she was thinking it. "You have no business here, so let's just go home. If you want to do something this summer, babysit."

"Well, we train the kids who volunteer here," Shadrach explained. "They catch on surprisingly fast." He placed the baby opossum back in the fleece bag. "Poor little guy. He's wondering, 'Where's Ma? What am I doing here? Where's nice, warm-loving Ma?' Some lunatic was doin' eighty miles an hour on a narrow country road with a forty-mile-per-hour speed limit. That's probably who killed Ma. It's not fair, but then who says anything's fair, huh?" For the first time since Chelsea met him, a harsh tone was in Shadrach's voice, but Chelsea understood why.

"Well, thank you so much for showing us around," Mom said, edging toward the door.

"Yeah, thanks," Chelsea echoed her mom. "I wanna work here if you'll let me."

"Okay," Shadrach agreed. "Go see Ms. Colbert in the science department at Tubman High, Chelsea. She coordinates all my volunteers. She's teaching summer school. She'll sign you up and give you permission slips and all that stuff. You'll come here with a group, and I'll train all you guys together."

"Thanks again! See ya," Chelsea cried. She trotted to keep up with Mom, who was almost running to the door.

When they got a few feet from the house, Mom shuddered. "Oh Chelsea, it smells so bad in there! I can't imagine working in a place like that!"

"I wouldn't mind it," Chelsea replied, getting into the car.

"Sweetheart," Mom finally admitted, "that man gives me the creeps. I would hate for you to have anything to do with him. I mean, I don't know anything about him, I admit it. But something's wrong with a man who lives in a ratty place like that and takes care of . . . those things all day."

"Mom," Chelsea objected, "lotsa people spend their lives caring for animals. I mean, they're living things too. This holy man—name was Francis—he lived in an Italian town called Assisi. He talked to animals and helped them. It was beautiful."

Mom shuddered again. "If you talk to animals you're . . . crazy, don't you think?" she asked. "I mean, of course it's all right to call your dog and stuff like that. But to feel so close to those little rat-like things. They're so hideous, Chelsea. I mean, just the whole idea of this badly scarred man and all the horrible little furry creatures . . . In a way, Inessa is right. It's like a horror movie."

"I bet Pop wouldn't feel that way," Chelsea stated suddenly. "I bet Pop would understand why I want to help Shadrach with the opossums."

Mom felt hurt. Both her children seemed in some frustrating way closer to their father than to her. Jaris tried hard to act as if he felt the same toward both his parents. But Mom could always tell that he was partial to his father's ideas and opinions. Pop could yell and shout and turn the whole house upside down with his tantrums. Still, his children looked at him as some sort of colorful, marvelous hero. Pop humiliated Chelsea in front of her friends over her skimpy clothing and brought her to tears. The next minute, he was her wonderful Pop who could do no wrong. Mom respected Chelsea's judgment in picking out her clothing but still couldn't gain that level of admiration.

That night, Pop came home dirtier and more tired than when he was working for old Jackson. He staggered straight to the bathroom to shower.

After a long shower, he shuffled from the bathroom and flopped into the easy chair in the living room.

"I'm gettin' a mechanic tomorrow to help me," he announced. "A great kid. He's got a lot of smarts. It's gonna be great, Monie. Kid's gonna be like me when Jackson was boss. Name's Boston Blake. I liked him right away. He reminds me of me when I was younger. Guts and know-how. Takes on those beaters like a pro. I tested him out. Spectacular."

"That's good, Lorenzo," Mom responded. "You've been working too hard trying to do it all yourself."

Chelsea came into the room. "You look tired, Pop," she remarked sitting on the arm of his chair. She leaned over and kissed him on the cheek.

"Oh baby!" Pop laughed. "That cheek ain't been shaved in three days. I didn't scratch your lips, did I little girl?"

"No, Pop," Chelsea answered. "Hey, can I ask you something?"

Before Chelsea could talk, Mom cut in. "Before Chelsea gives you some big story, Lorenzo, I want to tell you what happened today," Mom began. "There's this strange man, his name is Shadrach. He's, uh, very horrible looking, the poor man, with one eye, and he's badly scarred, I don't know why. But he spends his time caring for opossums—wounded ones, sick ones, babies. He lives in a stinky, rickety house on Indigo Street. Chelsea wants to go there and help him with these hideous little animals . . ."

"Oh man!" Pop responded. "That's quite a mouthful of words, babe. I am gettin' a very bad picture. I get this monster guy—let's call him ratman. He's king of all the creepy-crawlies, and our little girl wants to hang out with him. Is that the story, Chelsea?"

Chelsea cast her mother a hateful look, but she said nothing to her. "Pop," Chelsea explained, "Shadrach is a nice, kind man. He can't help that he was scarred in an explosion or something. He rescues wounded opossums and makes them well and returns them to the wild. He works with Ms. Colbert. She's gonna be my science teacher at Tubman when I'm a freshman. She recruits kids to go out to Shadrach's rescue center and help him. We get credit for doing it, and Ms. Colbert runs the whole deal. We go in a team from school. I maybe want to be a veterinarian, Pop, and this'll be a good thing for me."

Pop looked at Mom. "Babe," his eyebrows furrowed, "you were telling me a whole different story. I'm thinking now that the poor stiff isn't a pretty boy, so we're making him out to be the big bad wolf."

"No, Lorenzo," Mom struggled, "that's not the point at all!" He was doing it again.

He was making her look bad in front of her daughter.

"Pop, can I do it?" Chelsea pleaded, cutting to the chase. "Please, Pop, can I?"

"Hey little girl," Pop grinned at his daughter, "y'say this teacher at Tubman is in charge? And a whole group of you gonna be goin' over there, you know, to help these opossums out? Hey, what's wrong with that? I think it's all good. You could do a lot worse this summer. Go for it."

Chelsea looked at her mother as if to say, "See? Pop understands. He *always* understands. I don't know why you never do." No words were said, but Mom got the message.

"Thanks, Pop," Chelsea chirped, giving her father's prickly cheek another peck. Then she turned and marched to her room, her shoulders high.

CHAPTER THREE

Heston Crawford stared at Chelsea Spain as she got out of Jaris's car in the Harriet Tubman High School parking lot. "What're you doing here, Chelsea? Goin' to summer school?" he asked her.

"No," Chelsea answered, "I gotta see Ms. Colbert about working with opossums."

"Huh?" Heston asked. "Working with *what*?"

"There's this guy, his name is Shadrach," Chelsea explained. "He takes care of sick and wounded opossums, and he lets kids come and help him. Ms. Colbert arranges it. I gotta see her."

"No way!" Heston exclaimed. "For real?"

"Yeah," Chelsea replied, grinning. "Maybe you'd like to sign up too, Heston. It'd be fun working together."

"Wild animals are cool," Heston said.

Ms. Colbert came around the corner, smiling. "You guys look like this year's freshmen," she remarked.

"Yeah," Chelsea responded, "we graduated from Marian Anderson Middle School. We're gonna be going here to Tubman." The words sounded so good. Chelsea always thought it would be such a big deal to be going to Tubman High. This is where the big kids went, the kids who got to do almost-adult stuff. Chelsea knew she'd be only a lowly freshman, but just being here was going to be exciting. "Me and Heston want to help Shadrach with the opossums, and he said we had to sign up with you."

"Yeah," Ms. Colbert said, picking up her clipboard. "We've got a few kids already. We're going out to the opossum refuge on Saturday. If you guys are here

Saturday morning around ten, I can take you in my van."

Ms. Colbert gave Chelsea and Heston some papers for their parents to fill out. Then she wrote their names on her clipboard.

"Ms. Colbert," Chelsea asked, "do you know Shadrach real well?" She was hoping Ms. Colbert and Shadrach were good friends. It would help put Mom's fears to rest. Her mother was still uncomfortable about Chelsea helping out at the opossum refuge.

"Oh, we've worked together some," Ms. Colbert replied. "He's very patient with the volunteers. You'll learn a lot about the wild things. He's a very good man."

"Uh, I bet he was in the war. That's how he got hurt, huh?" Chelsea asked. If she could tell Mom that Shadrach was a wounded veteran that would go far in impressing her.

"Oh, you better ask Shadrach about that," Ms. Colbert answered evasively. "Okay, see you Saturday." Then she went into her classroom.

"How's the guy hurt?" Heston asked.

"He's missing an eye," Chelsea explained, "and his face is scarred on that side. It's like he was burned or something. That prissy old Inessa freaked out over him. She got stupid like he was a monster or something. Mom didn't like it either. She went to the opossum refuge with me, and she got weird. I was hopin' I could find out if he was a war hero. Then I coulda told her and Inessa so they'd be ashamed of looking down at him."

"Yeah, I bet he is," Heston said.

"Well, I gotta get back to my brother, Heston," Chelsea told him. "He's over there, pacing around in the parking lot. He gets antsy when he has to wait too long."

As Chelsea got close to Jaris's car, she heard loud music. "What's *that*, Jaris?" she yelled above the noise.

"It's music from Mali, you know, Africa," Jaris answered. "It's rock and funk, West African. It's got this awesome guitar sound with blues and boogie mixed in."

Jaris loved music. He was always looking for something unusual. "Well, you signed up for the opossum deal, chili pepper?"

"Yeah. Heston was there, and he signed up too," Chelsea told him. "That's extra nice 'cause we can work together."

They got into the car, and Jaris tuned the music down. It was now playing at a low background level. He started the Honda and steered for the exit to the lot.

"You know what, Jare?" Chelsea mused. "I hope Tubman is gonna be as great as I think. I mean, I hope I make a lotta nice friends. Like I don't have as many really good friends as you had when you were a freshman. You came from middle school with guys like Trevor and Derrick, Alonee, Sereeta, Sami. Y'know, that little bunch Sami calls 'Alonee's posse.' I mean, you guys're tight. Except for Athena and Keisha and maybe Heston, I haven't got anybody. Inessa's too prissy. You can't have any fun with her. Athena's always pushing me farther than I wanna go, but she's so fun."

45

"You'll make new friends, chili pepper," Jaris assured her.

"I hope," Chelsea wished, staring straight ahead through the windshield. "There's some mean girls coming from middle school too, girls like Kanika and Hana. They used to get all the girls together in eighth grade. They'd make them all swear they wouldn't talk to a certain girl—*at all*. They'd just freeze someone out and pretend she didn't exist. It was a game with them, a really cruel game."

Jaris glanced at his sister. "They ever do that to you, Chelsea?"

"Yeah," his sister admitted. "One whole week, nobody would talk to me, except for Athena. It was horrible. I'd ask somebody something, and they'd pretend they didn't hear me. Nobody would eat lunch with me, but Athena did."

"Why did they do that?" Jaris asked. Jaris always felt that girls could often be meaner than boys. If a boy didn't like you, he might punch you in the nose. The next minute you'd be friends again.

Chelsea shrugged. "'Cause they're mean. I guess it made them feel big that they could control other people. Kanika, especially. Kanika Brewster isn't very pretty, but she's got power. She gets Hana to do her dirty work. I hope they're not in any of my classes."

"Don't worry about them," Jaris advised. "You got other friends who aren't starting high school yet, like Lark Lennox, Kayla Shaw, and Maya Archer. You can have fun with them."

Chelsea made a face. "Oh but Jaris, they're little kids!" she objected. "I can't hang out with middle schoolers! That's so lame. They're like babies, and I'm in senior high school!"

"Come on, chili pepper," Jaris laughed. "They're like a year or two behind you!" He turned into the driveway of the Spain house.

"Look, Pop's truck," Jaris pointed. "He's home in the middle of the day. I hope nothing's wrong."

"He's the boss now, Jaris," Chelsea said. "He can come home anytime he wants."

As Chelsea and Jaris came into the house, they heard their parents talking in the living room. It wasn't an argument, but neither was it a pleasant conversation. They were seated at either end of the sofa.

"You just continually make me look bad to the children," Mom was saying. "Especially to Chelsea about those stupid little rats she wants to befriend."

"Okay, babe," Pop responded. "Let's discuss stuff together before it turns into a big deal. I agree with that. But it ain't any good for me either to come home from work and get hit with some loony story. Way you were talkin', some rat keeper who looks like Frankenstein's monster wanted our daughter to work in his lab. So before you come on so strong to Chelsea, let's you and me hash it out, babe. Let's not start with the hysteria, okay?"

"I'm never hysterical," Mom objected crossly. "I'm a very rational person."

"Yeah, yeah," Pop agreed. "But you're throwing around words like 'horrible looking man in a rickety house.' I'm getting' images in my mind of some wacko from the Halloween movies. That ain't very rational, babe."

Mom's silence seemed to be her way of saying, "Conversation over." Pop waited a few seconds to make sure he got the message right. He then leaned back.

"Anyway, getting back to the garage," he said. "Boston's doing fine, but I gotta watch the kid. He'll be jerking some part out of one of the beaters, and it ain't even what's wrong. I gotta make sure he's doin' it right. He took that course at the community college in mechanics and that's great. But I learned by doing. I was working on engines with my own pop when I was eight years old." Pop laughed. "He's kind of scared of me. He knows I know my stuff. But he'll be okay."

"Just don't turn into old Jackson, Lorenzo," Mom warned. "You know how you felt about him."

Pop laughed again. "Yeah, you're right, Monie. But now that I think back on it, Jackson was okay. I hated his guts when he was riding me, but I learned a lot from him. He was all right."

Pop turned and saw Chelsea in the doorway. "How's it goin', little girl?" he asked.

"Good," Chelsea replied. "But I'm a little nervous about finding good friends at Tubman when I start there. I mean, except for Athena and Inessa, I got no real friends."

Pop's bushy eyebrows went up. "Oh boy—Athena—she's the top of the list now?" he remarked. "You are in trouble, little girl."

"Oh, Inessa is such a Goody Two-shoes," Chelsea admitted. "And, yeah,

Athena is a little wild. There's something wrong with all of them . . ."

"Lissen to her," Pop crowed. "Our little girl is gettin' the big head. She's growin' into a little woman, and now the head is swellin' up. Here's some good advice, Chelsea. Make friends with the shy little twerps who got no friends. Stay away from the cliques, the popular chicks. They're usually creeps. You hang with them, you'll get just like them."

Mom had a skeptical look on her face.

Pop looked at Jaris and spoke to him. "You been there, boy. It's a zoo, right? You got the tigers and the monkeys clowning around and the poor little shy ones. Some of those popular girls got claws like tigers. They like to tear people apart. You don't want nothin' to do with them. High school can be a terrible place. You're trapped there with a bunch of weirdoes, and you can't get away."

"Don't let your father scare you, Chelsea," Mom advised. "Most of the kids in your freshman class will be nice and friendly." She glanced at Jaris for support. "Isn't that so, Jaris?" she asked.

Jaris cleared his throat. He wanted to make Mom feel good and agree with her. He tried to forget about Marko Lane and Jasmine Benson. "Yeah, Mom," he granted, "most of them are okay."

Pop grabbed a soda and headed back to the garage. He turned his radio up loud. He loved jazz, and the music was so loud it seemed the air itself rattled. Pop didn't care. The pickup truck disappeared down the street.

"Mom," Chelsea remarked suddenly. "I bet you were really popular in high school. I mean you're smart and pretty. I bet you had no trouble making friends."

Mom flushed. She wasn't used to such nice compliments from her daughter, especially lately. "Thank you, Chelsea, that's sweet," Mom said. "I had a lot of fun in ninth grade."

"Weren't there ever any mean girls?" Chelsea asked.

Mom smiled weakly. "Well, this girl Marion," she explained, "she had a boyfriend. I made the mistake of talking to him at a beach party. I didn't even know he was her boyfriend. She and two of her friends followed me into the restroom later on. They cornered me in there. They pulled my hair, and they ripped my new T-shirt. They punched me. I was so scared."

"What'd you do then?" Chelsea asked eagerly. "Did you and your friends get them back?"

"Oh no, Chelsea!" Mom objected. "That's wrong. I didn't want to get a big fight going. I just totally avoided them after that."

Chelsea looked disappointed. She and Jaris went down the hallway. Partway to their rooms, she remarked, "If some girls beat me up like that, I'd get them back."

Jaris grinned. "That'd feel good," he advised. "But it wouldn't make things better. But listen, chili pepper. Anybody gives you trouble at Tubman, you got somebody to help you, okay? I got your back, chili pepper. Don't you ever forget that."

Chelsea grinned and gave Jaris a quick hug.

Jaris went into his own room to read over the AP American History material. Ms. McDowell had passed it out at the end of his junior year. Jaris wanted badly to get into a really great class and do well, but he had doubts. He kept on wondering whether he could compete with people like Oliver Randall, Alonee Lennox, or even Sereeta. He always thought Sereeta was smarter than him. In fact, Jaris thought everybody in the class would be smarter than him. He made good grades, but he worked harder than anybody else he knew.

Jaris's cell phone rang. "Hello, Jaris?" said Sereeta, Jaris's girlfriend. She didn't sound happy. Jaris had loved Sereeta ever since middle school. But she didn't return his feelings until the middle of their junior year. Sereeta's divorced and remarried parents didn't want her around for many of her teenaged years. Now she lived with her grandmother, and that was better. But she was constantly reaching out to her mother, looking for a closer relationship. A few weeks ago, Sereeta and her mother took a wonderful trip to San Francisco, and Sereeta was overjoyed. For a little while, she had a mother again, but Jaris feared it wouldn't last.

"Hey Sereeta, what's up?" Jaris asked, fearing the answer. He hoped against hope that she was just looking to get together with him, if just for an hour or two. They often sneaked off together to the beach.

"Jaris, are you really busy?" Sereeta asked.

"Uh no. I don't go to work at the Chicken Shack for a few hours. Why?" Jaris responded.

"I hate to ask you to do this, Jaris," she murmured. "But I didn't know who else to call. My mom, she's a little bit . . . you know, sick. She's downtown, and she misplaced her wallet. She's like stuck in this restaurant, and they're giving her a hard time. She just called me on my cell phone, Jaris," Sereeta's voice broke a little. "Mom was crying. The people there, they're talking about calling the police and stuff. I just don't know what to do, Jaris, but I really hate dragging you into this."

"Sereeta, listen, take it easy," Jaris assured her. Jaris's brain started spinning. Sereeta's mother had a serious drinking problem, and it kept getting worse. She swore she was getting help. She even said she was attending meetings, and they were helping her.

Poor Sereeta, Jaris thought. How making this call must have humiliated her. How it must have torn her apart. "Sereeta, I'll pick you up right away at your grandma's house," Jaris told his girl. "We'll go down and give your mom a ride home, okay? Just take it easy."

"Thank you, Jaris," Sereeta sighed. "Grandma's car is in the shop again. I have no way of . . . I'm so sorry to be asking this." Her voice broke again.

"No, no, don't worry about it, babe. I'm leaving right now," Jaris told her. He grabbed the keys to his car and rushed down the hall.

Mom saw him. "Honey, you look upset. Is everything all right?" she asked.

"Yeah, Mom," Jaris replied, stopping in his tracks for a second. "Sereeta's mom got stranded downtown. She, uh, misplaced her purse or something. We're picking her up." Then he was out the door. Mom had a strange, knowing look in her eyes, but she said nothing, mercifully.

No way in the world did Jaris want to tell Mom what was really going on, even though Mom suspected. Everyone in town knew that Olivia Manley, Sereeta's mom, was a drunk. Still, Jaris wanted to give the woman a shred of privacy and dignity now that she had fallen one more time.

CHAPTER FOUR

Sereeta was waiting in the front yard of her grandmother's house. She ran to Jaris's car and got in.

"Thank you so much, Jaris," she sighed in a small, hurt voice. "I didn't even tell Grandma what was going on. She doesn't like Mom anyway. She never did. Since Mom divorced her son, she's almost hated her. Oh Jaris!" Sereeta began to cry.

"It's okay, babe," Jaris assured her. "We'll be downtown in no time."

"She's at the Green Hornet Café on Main Street," Sereeta told him.

"Yeah, I know where that is," Jaris nodded. "It's near the civic center where the

Purple Rave Rappers came last spring. Me and Trevor caught that."

"Perry, my stepfather, he's out of town," Sereeta explained. "He's been on a business trip. She gets so lonely that she starts drinking."

"Where's Jake?" Jaris asked. Jake was the baby son of Olivia and Perry Manley. He was Sereeta's stepbrother.

"The baby is almost living full-time with a nanny. Mom has less and less to do with Jake," Sereeta answered.

"We'll be there in no time," Jaris declared. He couldn't begin to imagine what it was like for Sereeta. His heart ached for her. Jaris was so proud of his parents. Pop was a strong, dependable man, and Mom was a highly respected teacher in the community. Jaris shuddered to think of how Sereeta was feeling. What was it like to get a phone call that your mother is drunk in a bar? How must it feel to think your mom might be arrested for public drunkenness?

Jaris pulled into the parking lot behind the Green Hornet Café. Jaris and Sereeta went in together, and they spotted Olivia Manley over in a corner booth. She was resting her head in her hands, her elbows on the table. Sereeta went to her mother. Jaris went over to the manager, who had watched them come in.

"Hey man," Jaris told him, "we're picking up her mom right now." He nodded toward Mrs. Manley in the booth.

"Good," the manager responded. "We offered to call a cab for her, but she said she had no money left. She wasn't even sure where she lived. She came in here, and we served her a few drinks. Then she struck up a conversation with some guy. He gave her some of his drinks, and then she got smashed. I think she was drinking before she got here."

The manager seemed sympathetic. "Anyway," he went on, "the other guy—the louse—he took off. We dunno. Then she wanted more to drink and got a little nasty with the waitress. Things got loud for a while. We couldn't get her to leave. We thought we might have to call the cops. Lucky she had her daughter's cell number programmed into her phone. She made the call and then just put her head down and conked out."

The manager nodded over to the booth as he spoke. "It's too bad," he remarked, "a pretty, nicely dressed woman like that."

"We owe you anything, man?" Jaris asked.

"Nope," the manager replied. "She paid as she went. She just ran outta cash. Claims she lost her purse. . . . Well, good luck to you and your girlfriend."

By the time Jaris walked over to the booth, Olivia Manley was standing, though she leaned on Sereeta's arm. "I do not know what is going on here," the woman declared. She struggled to speak clearly, without slurring. "Everything was going perfectly well when my purse was stolen. I would like to know who . . . who took my purse."

Sereeta put her arm around her mother. "We're going home, Mom," she spoke softly to her. "I have your purse. It was under the table. Now we're taking you home."

"Mrs. Manley," Jaris asked, "is your car in the lot?"

The woman stared at Jaris and blinked a couple of times. She was trying to remember how she got to the café.

"I took the trolley here," Mrs. Manley finally replied. "It was all going perfectly well." The woman swung her gaze to her daughter. "I insist on knowing what . . . what happened."

With help from her daughter and Jaris, Sereeta's mother made it to Jaris's car and got into the back seat. Sereeta buckled her in and sat in the back with her.

"Perry's gone, you know. He suddenly upped and left," Mrs. Manley stated. "I would like to know why."

"He's on a business trip, Mom," Sereeta explained.

"A business trip indeed! That's a likely story!" she scoffed. "He's been gone for weeks."

"No Mom, just a couple days," Sereeta insisted. "He'll be home soon, maybe tonight."

As they drove, Sereeta told Jaris, "Just drop me off at Mom's house. I'll stay with her until Perry gets back."

"Sereeta, when he gets home, call me," Jaris instructed her. "And I'll take you home to your grandmother's house. If I'm at the Chicken Shack, I'll quit early. Neal's good about stuff like that."

"You've done enough for me, Jaris," Sereeta insisted.

"Please call me when Perry gets home," Jaris repeated. "If it's early, we can hang for a while, Sereeta, and just unwind. I need to be with you tonight for a little while if it's possible, babe. I think you need to be with me too."

"Okay," Sereeta responded in a hushed voice. "Jaris, you're wonderful."

"No, I'm not," Jaris objected. "I just love you, babe."

"Me too," Sereeta whispered, but Jaris heard her.

Jaris pulled into the driveway of the Manley home. Sereeta had lived there with her mother and stepfather before she moved to her grandmother's. Jaris and Sereeta helped her mother out of the car and into the house. She kept protesting that she didn't need any help before flopping heavily into a reclining chair.

"You sure you'll be okay?" Jaris asked Sereeta.

"Yeah, fine," Sereeta assured him.

"And you'll call me, promise?" Jaris asked.

Jaris took his girl into his arms and kissed her.

Sereeta nodded yes. "I promise," Sereeta told him.

Mrs. Manley sat in the chair, watching the two of them. Her almost seventeen-year-old daughter was in the living room,

kissing a handsome boy. "Sereeta," she exclaimed in a thick voice. "I didn' know you
had a boyfrien'. Since when . . . when did
you have a boyfrien'?"

"See you later, babe," Jaris whispered to
her, and he left.

Jaris felt terrible down to his bones. He
drove to the Chicken Shack for his shift, but
he had really wanted to stay with Sereeta.
Still, he couldn't have done much good. No
doubt, when Perry Manley got home, there
would be an argument, perhaps an ugly
fight. Sereeta didn't want Jaris to see that.
She was humiliated enough.

Jaris loved Sereeta so much, and her
mother's drinking was tearing her apart.
One day the woman was sober and pleasant; the next day she had drunk herself into
a stupor. Last year, Sereeta, her friends,
and their mothers had arranged to give
Olivia Manley a beautiful birthday party.
Sereeta's mother was too drunk to come.
But then on the trip to San Francisco, she
was fine. Sereeta felt as though she was

living on a roller coaster. Sereeta's mother kept promising to get help, but instead she was spiraling deeper and deeper into an abyss.

Trevor Jenkins was already working at the Chicken Shack when Jaris got there. Trevor was just about Jaris's closest friend. The two boys would do anything for each other. Trevor's dad had long ago abandoned the family. Since then, his mother had raised him and three older boys alone by working long hours as a nurse's aide.

"Man," Trevor commented to Jaris, "you look like you just got run over by a big rig."

Jaris slipped on his yellow and white Chicken Shack shirt and joined Trevor at the counter. "Sereeta's mom got sick downtown, and we had to go pick her up," he explained grimly. "It's tearing Sereeta apart."

Trevor shook his head. "I feel for you, man," he sympathized.

"I want to help Sereeta, but what can I do?" Jaris said.

"With us it was easier," Trevor remarked. "When Pa was drunk all the time, Ma threw him out. She's tough. She cut off all contact with him. She raised us clean. Any one of us had turned to booze, she woulda beat the living daylights outta us. That sucka woulda had a long sleep. It's bad with Sereeta that it's up and down like that."

"Sereeta still loves her mom," Jaris commented. "She can't just forget about her. Most of the time Sereeta's mom doesn't even seem to care if her daughter's on earth. Now she's doing the same thing with the baby—Jake. But Sereeta's clinging to the idea of a fantasy mom. You shoulda seen her tonight, dude. She was so embarrassed and worried, she looked sick."

"I'm sorry, bro," Trevor consoled his friend. "Booze is an awful, awful drug. Most people don't see it like that. Most deadly auto wrecks, that's booze at work. Most times when husbands kill their wives or girlfriends, they're drunk. It's a bad thing, Jaris."

"Yeah," Jaris agreed. "My pop used to drink a little too much when he'd get stressed. Then he went down to Pastor Bromley's church, and he took the pledge to stop drinking. I was so proud of him for doing that. He just did it on the spur of the moment. It was to honor the memory of a young girl who was killed by a drunk driver. It's made such a difference in our house. It's so good for Mom and me and Chelsea. It's like something was hanging over our heads, and now it's gone."

A couple of customers entered the store, and the two boys had to get to work.

Sereeta called Jaris about ten minutes before quitting time. Perry had arrived home. Finding his wife drunk, he had flown into a rage. The husband and wife were having a terrible argument, but at least Sereeta could go home.

Jaris quit a little early with his boss Neal's okay. He headed for the Manley house to pick up Sereeta. She was standing in the driveway, waiting for him, and she got into the car quickly.

"You okay, babe?" Jaris asked.

"Yeah. They're quiet now," Sereeta answered. "Mom went to bed, and he's watching TV. What a night!" She was shaking her head. "I don't know what I would have done without you tonight, Jaris. My mom might be in jail right now."

Jaris didn't know what to say. He'd gone over all the options in his own mind. There was no good one. He might tell Sereeta that her mother was just a lost cause. He could urge her to forget about her mom. He could argue that Sereeta's life shouldn't be ruined like this. But that wouldn't fly. You can't stop loving somebody because it's the smart thing to do. That's not what love is about.

"Let's stop for a mocha," Jaris suggested.

"It won't make you too late, will it?" Sereeta asked.

"No, we won't be long," Jaris responded. "I'll be home at pretty much the regular time."

They stopped at a little coffee shop and sat in a rear booth. It was a warm night. The hot summer sun had gone down, but the heavy humid air remained. The chilled mocha hit the spot.

"My little sister ran into this guy, Shadrach," Jaris told his girl. "He rescues opossums. She and a friend are gonna volunteer at his rescue shelter." Jaris was desperate to change the subject from what this terrible night was all about.

"Oh I've seen him," Sereeta replied. "One night I was with my grandma, and he was by the side of the road scooping up a poor little wounded opossum. We didn't know what was going on, and we stopped. He told us the opossum may not survive its injuries, but at least it would die comfortably without suffering. We were so touched. I think it's wonderful for Chelsea to get involved in that. They're only little wild things, but they have feelings too. Who's to say they don't have a claim on our mercy?"

Jaris was surprised that Sereeta didn't mention anything about Shadrach's startling physical appearance. That was the first thing most people noticed. But that was Sereeta. She had so much love and compassion in her that external things didn't matter so much.

That was why Sereeta could see a mother who seemed hardly to care for her. And the girl could still focus on the heartbreaking truth that the woman was her mother.

That was why Sereeta could see her mother disheveled, slipping into spells of shameful drunkenness, and still love her.

That was why Sereeta could ignore Shadrach's missing eye and facial scars. She could see only the compassion of a good man who wanted to stop suffering wherever he found it.

Jaris was overwhelmed with love and admiration for this girl. He wanted to put his arms around her and protect her from everything that might hurt her in any way.

And he felt upset that he couldn't protect her against what hurt her most of all.

"I'm pretty sure I'll be taking Ms. McDowell's AP American History class when school starts, Sereeta. You're taking it, aren't you?" Jaris asked.

"Yeah," Sereeta replied. "I took AP Calculus and that worked out. I like the idea of getting college credit while I'm still in high school. It's like getting a jump on college."

"Oliver and Alonee are taking it too," Jaris added. "But you guys are all smarter than me. I'm getting cold feet."

"Oh Jaris, you underestimate yourself. You'll do fine," Sereeta assured him. "Did you know Marko Lane is taking it too?"

"You gotta be kidding!" Jaris groaned. Marko Lane and his girlfriend, Jasmine Benson, made a hobby of disrupting classes at Tubman High, but they were afraid of Ms. McDowell. They didn't dare mess with her.

"No, Marko's pretty smart when he tries," Sereeta stated. "He usually goofs off, but he's determined to ace this class. Remember when he brought his father over to watch the race, and he was beaten? He thinks getting AP credit will give him something to make it up to his father and impress him."

They finished their icy drinks and headed for Sereeta's grandmother's house. When they got there, Jaris came in for just a minute to say hello to Mrs. Prince.

"I been a little worried, girl," Bessie Prince scolded. "You ain't often this late."

"I'm sorry, Grandma. I should've called," Sereeta apologized.

Bessie Prince looked at Jaris and smiled. "I see you were in good hands, child," she told her granddaughter. "This is a very fine boy. Mighty handsome too."

"Thank you, ma'am," Jaris said. He liked Bessie Prince. She was a good, down-to-earth, caring woman. She came from another generation when people were more willing to sacrifice.

"Sereeta has told me all about you, Jaris," the older woman continued. "I met your mama, Monica Spain, at the grocery store the other day. She was so nice. She helped me load all my groceries in my car. I see where your kind ways come from, boy."

Then the smile faded from the woman's face, and she spoke to Sereeta. "Your mama at it again, eh, darlin'?"

Sereeta seemed taken aback. She didn't think her grandmother knew anything about this latest incident.

"She called here, child," Bessie Prince explained. "She had this number. I tol' her you weren't here. She got you on your cell phone, I suppose. She was in a bad way. The barkeep or somebody come on the phone. He say somebody better come get her pretty quick."

Jaris and Sereeta exchanged a sad look.

"She got me, Grandma, and Jaris drove me down to pick her up," Sereeta explained.

Bessie Prince looked at Jaris and spoke to him. "You need to talk some sense into this chil', young fella. In this world there are such things as lost causes. You gotta look at 'em straight in the eye, and face the truth. Lordy, I tried with all my might to love Olivia Sanders when my son brought her around as his girlfriend. I could see right from the start that she'd be nothing but heartache for my boy. But there was no convincing him. She's beautiful. She *was* beautiful anyway. Don't know as to how she looks now. Booze takes its toll."

Jaris looked at the old woman sympathetically. He knew she was going through the same pain he was. Somebody they both loved—Sereeta—was paying the price for Olivia Manley's failures.

"This poor chil' here," Bessie Prince went on, "my only grandchild. I want for her to have a good life. I'm an old woman. The only light in my life right now is to think that this child will have a good life. Jaris Spain, you take care of her. Take care of my little Sereeta. Try to talk some sense into her. She ain' got no mama. No way. No how. She need to stop chasing after a mirage. It looks like water shinin' in the desert, but it's not water at all. It's a cruel hoax. Same with Sereeta's mom. She's no mama no more. Maybe she never was. Sereeta, she need to stop grabbing at the mirage. She'll only find a handful of dust to break her heart."

Sereeta stood there in the middle of the room, the tears running down her face. What her grandmother was saying rang true. Sereeta knew that, but it didn't make any difference. There were times—brief, bright, even glorious times, like when Sereeta and her mother went to San Francisco. At those times, Olivia Manley was a wonderful mother again. Glimpses of what she had been and might be again kept

Sereeta hoping. Her mother never sank into a perpetual state of alcohol stupor, as Trevor Jenkins' father had. If she had, maybe Sereeta could have put her out of her life. But the normal interludes kept the girl's hope alive.

CHAPTER FIVE

Mattie Archer drove her daughter, Lark Lennox, and Chelsea Spain to the Ice House for frozen yogurt. Maya Archer was a year younger than Chelsea. She was going to be at Marian Anderson Middle School another year.

Mattie Archer saw a friend and went to talk with her, leaving the girls alone.

"I wish you guys were coming to Tubman right away," Chelsea told Maya and Lark.

"I got two more years of middle school," Lark groaned. "It's gonna be even more awful with you gone, Chel."

Suddenly two more girls appeared. They'd been in eighth grade at Anderson,

but they weren't Chelsea's friends. Kanika
Brewster and Hana Ray came over with
sneers on their faces. "I heard you were
gonna work with that weirdo who takes
care of dirty opossums, Chelsea," Kanika
said.

"So what?" Chelsea snapped.

"That Shadrach guy, I bet he got hurt in
a gang fight up in LA," Hana remarked.

"I don't believe that," Chelsea told the
girl. "I think he's a war veteran, and he got
hurt over there in Iraq or Afghanistan."

Kanika and Hana both laughed. Kanika
crowed, "You're so brainless, girl. You
think this weirdo woulda been taken in the
army? They only take smart guys like my
father. He was in the army, and he's got tons
of medals. It's a volunteer army, and only
the best guys can come in a volunteer army.
They never woulda wanted that old
Shadrach."

"The army recruiter woulda chased
Shadrach away," Hana chimed in. Hana
tried to copy everything Kanika did.

Chelsea felt sorry for Hana having a role model as creepy as Kanika. "He's a weirdo who's got nothing better to do than pick up old dead opossums. That is really dangerous 'cause they all got rabies."

"Shows how much you know," Chelsea countered. "Opossums can't get rabies 'cause their body temperatures are too low."

"Liar!" Kanika yelled shrilly. "You just made that up."

"Everybody knows opossums have rabies," Hana said loyally.

"You girls are kinda mean," Maya Archer commented.

"I don't like you," Lark Lennox agreed. "Go away."

"Chelsea Spain, why you hanging with these little babies?" Kanika demanded, looking scornfully at Maya and Lark. "And, anyway, you're so stupid you woulda flunked science at Anderson if Heston Crawford didn't help you!"

Suddenly Mattie Archer was standing there, her hands on her ample hips. "Kanika

Brewster, what're you hollerin' about?" she demanded. "You're a troublemaker Kanika, and so are you, Hana. You goin' to Tubman now, and they make short work of trouble-makers there. Y'hear what I'm sayin'? You may be queen of the meanies at Anderson Middle School, but you playin' in a bigger pool now, girl. Tubman freshman, they got no time for fools like you, Kanika. And Hana, you best get a mind of your own before you turn out as bad as Kanika! Next time I see your ma in the supermarket, Hana, I'm gonna ask her. I'm gonna find out why you hangin' with Kanika and doin' everythin' she tell you to do. You need to be your own self."

Kanika and Hana grabbed their frozen yogurt cones and marched out of the Ice House.

On Saturday morning, Jaris dropped Chelsea off at Tubman High. Pop was rid-ing with them this morning, and Jaris was dropping him at work. His pickup needed a new battery. Ms. Colbert was already at school, loading up her van.

"Have fun with the opossums, little girl," Pop sang. "I'd rather you made friends with the opossums than most kids your age, if you get my meaning."

Chelsea saw Athena and Heston standing by Ms. Colbert's van. Chelsea rushed over. "Athena! You said you weren't interested in working with the opossums!" she said.

"I changed my mind," Athena answered. "Summer's barely going, and I'm already bored outta my mind. Mom is after me to start reading all these ghastly books, like about some dude named *Ivanhoe*. I mean, it's summer! I'm supposed to be having fun. All of a sudden the opossums sounded good."

"I'm glad you came," Chelsea responded happily.

Maurice Moore came biking up. When he saw Chelsea, he said, "Hey Chel, how's that freakin' lunatic brother of yours? He still terrorizing kids in the 'hood?"

Chelsea laughed. Jaris had run Maurice off their property when he was wrestling with Athena in the front yard. "Jaris is okay," she assured him. "He just wants a little respect."

"That dude is crazeee," Maurice whistled.

"Yeah," Heston admitted, "he scares me too."

"I didn't think you'd be here, Maurice," Chelsea remarked. Maurice was a tough, trash-talking, soon-to-be freshman. He once bragged to some friends that he went tagging one time with the Nite Ryders just to see what it was like. He even helped them boost some beer from the supermarket parking lot.

"I like that dude, Shadrach," Maurice replied. "He's pretty cool. Anyway, this work sounds weird enough to be interesting. My old man had me doing chores around the house, and that's the pits, man. My father's a tyrant. 'Go there, do this,' twenty-four-seven. Weed the stinkin' yard. Paint the stinkin' fence. I told him I could do this and get credit for science in school, and he let me go. He really wants me to do good at Tubman. I got mostly Ds at Anderson."

"Okay!" Ms. Colbert announced as she looked up from her clipboard. "We got everybody who signed up. Chelsea, Athena, Maurice, and Heston. You'll all be in my science class at Tubman when school starts. That's my Intro to Science for ninth grade. If you keep a good journal about your experiences here with the opossum rescue program, you'll get credit."

They all piled into the teacher's van. Chelsea was happy and excited. She was with her friends, and they were going to do something both good and exciting.

"I never met Shadrach," Athena commented. "Is it true that he's a one-eyed pirate?"

Ms. Colbert heard the comment and laughed. "Don't worry, Athena," she assured the girl, "we've checked Shadrach out quite thoroughly. We found no convictions for piracy on the high seas."

"He *looks* like a pirate though, huh, Chelsea?" Heston asked. "You've seen him."

"You guys," Ms. Colbert cautioned, "don't be asking Shadrach a lot of silly questions about his injuries, okay? I imagine he gets enough of that. When you get to know him better, he may share his story with you. Let him do it in his own time."

Chelsea liked Ms. Colbert. She seemed really cool. It was reassuring to Chelsea that she already had good rapport with one of the teachers she would have at Tubman. It made thinking about the first day of school less scary.

As they turned onto Indigo Street, Ms. Colbert forewarned the students. "I know you've been here already, Chelsea. But for the rest of you, be prepared for a very simple, no-frills place. Shadrach keeps it clean and orderly for the rescued opossums. But you're not going to see gleaming facilities like at a modern zoo. The zoo has tax money. Shadrach relies on his own income and donations."

"Why does he do this stuff?" Maurice asked. "My dad says nothin' is worth doin' if you don't get paid."

Ms. Colbert glanced back at Maurice. "Maurice, we do a lot in life we don't get paid for. There are other forms of compensation, like satisfaction. Shadrach cares about the animals he rescues. It makes him happy to get them well and release them back into the wild. I went with him and some kids for a night release of an opossum. I'm telling you guys, it was a very emotional experience."

Maurice didn't say anything, but he still thought this Shadrach had to be crazy. "The place looks like a dump," Maurice remarked as they pulled into the driveway.

"Maurice," Ms. Colbert scolded, "you'll be representing Tubman. Be careful what you say. We don't want to make our school look bad. We don't want

Shadrach to think our kids have no manners. Okay?"

"Sorry," Maurice assented. "I'm cool."

All five of them went to the door, and Shadrach swung it wide. "Hi there!" Shadrach greeted them. "Come on in."

Ms. Colbert introduced the four Tubman students. Then she announced, "I'll be back around noon to pick you guys up if that works for you, Shadrach."

"Fine," he agreed, "two hours is perfect for the tour and for beginning training."

When Ms. Colbert left, Shadrach said, "Okay. I'll show you the cages where we keep the adult opossums and the plastic containers for the babies."

"Do you *really* like doing this stuff, Mr. Shadrach?" Maurice asked.

"Shadrach is fine. No 'mister' necessary," Shadrach told the boy. "And, yeah, I love it."

"When Chelsea told me about this place," Athena remarked, "I went on the Internet, and I found out some interesting stuff about opossums. They've been in North America for like a hundred and twenty million years. I thought that was amazing. I mean, a lot of nerve we humans have pushing them out of their habitat, huh?"

Shadrach smiled at Athena. "I like the way this girl thinks," he announced to the small group. "We humans are pretty arrogant when it comes to pushing other species out of the way. Opossums are quite smart. They're smarter than dogs. They've been given tests to prove that. In their natural habitat, they've got plenty of food, plants, insects, but in our 'hood,' they gotta be resourceful. They eke out a living between houses, behind fences. They depend on stuff like cat food, cockroaches, and rats. In spite of big, nasty dogs, automobiles, and bigger, nastier people, they thrive."

"What *good* are they?" Heston asked.

Shadrach paused. He turned and looked at Heston. "What good is anybody? That's not for us to figure out. They *are*. Opossums are. There's a reason for any of us to survive. We just don't always know the reason."

The four teenagers looked into the cages and seemed especially fascinated by Magic. "Who wants to hold him?" Shadrach asked.

Athena jumped back. "Not me," she protested.

"Chelsea held him the other day," Shadrach urged. "He liked her."

"He's so cute and lovable," Chelsea remarked. "He feels like a kitten."

"Maybe I'll hold him next time," Heston responded.

Maurice stepped closer to the cage. He peered in at the little animal with the bright, beady eyes. "I'd like to take a shot at holding him," Maurice declared.

Shadrach opened the cage and put Magic in Maurice's arms. Magic looked intently up at the boy. Maurice had a strange look on his face. "He's lookin' at me like he's tryin' to figure me out," Maurice commented.

"Probably that's what he's doing," Shadrach said.

"But animals can't figure things out like we do, can they?" Athena asked.

"How do you know?" Shadrach asked with a quizzical smile.

Athena shrugged. "Yeah," she agreed with a nod of her head.

"That guy there—Magic," Shadrach told them, "he's getting stronger every day. I go special places when I release them at night. He's getting ready to go. I'll miss him, but he wants to go. They all do. A cage is no better for an animal than it is for a person. Any of you kids still with the program, you can come with me and watch the release. You'll never forget it."

"Ms. Colbert told us she was with you when you released an opossum. She said it was wonderful," Chelsea remarked. "I'd love to see that."

Shadrach put Magic back into his cage. Then he put the four teenagers to work replacing the old wet newspaper in the cages with fresh newspaper. At first Athena and Heston were saying "Yuck" and grimacing, but then they got in the swing of things. They became very efficient. Chelsea and Maurice put fresh newspapers in the plastic bin for the baby opossums. "Look at them," Maurice gasped with a kind of awe in his voice. "They're so tiny, like little worms or something, but they got big ears!"

Chelsea smiled at Maurice. She knew Maurice since they both started at Marian Anderson Middle School. Maurice disrupted class a lot. He was a wild kid. He was usually bored, and when he was bored, he made trouble. He got poor grades, and he talked trash. When he was mad, every other word from his mouth was something they wouldn't allow on TV. Chelsea had seen him get into fights too, but always off school grounds so he wasn't busted. It seemed strange to see him now so fascinated with these little animals.

Twelve o'clock came too quickly. Shadrach made sure everybody washed their hands thoroughly a few minutes before Ms. Colbert's van appeared.

"Well, for those of you not too grossed out, see you next Saturday. Thanks for coming over and helping out today. You were all great," Shadrach complimented them.

Chelsea looked more closely at the man than she had before. His one eye was deep, dark blue. His features were nice. He had a rather broad nose and full expressive lips. For a second, she tried to imagine what he looked like before the accident. He probably was handsome. He would have looked like Will Smith as a young man. Chelsea thought maybe Shadrach was from Louisiana because she knew some other black people with blue eyes from there.

"Thanks for having us, Shadrach," Chelsea responded.

When the four of them were in the van, Ms. Colbert asked, "How'd it go?"

"It's dirty work," Athena answered. "I hated it at first, but then I got used to it. I really like Shadrach. I got to sorta like the little opossums too."

"It was good," Heston added. "I got a lot of stuff to put in my journal. I learned a lot."

"I loved it," Chelsea said. "I knew I would, but it was even better than I thought. The opossums are so cute. And Shadrach is way cool."

"I guess I'll come back next week," Maurice concluded. "I want to see what happens to that guy—Magic. He looked at me real funny, like he knew stuff about me. I don't know, but I think he's probably an outsider in the opossum community too. He's kinda, you know, like me."

"Well, it sounds like everybody is coming back next Saturday?" Ms. Colbert asked. "And more kids may be joining. Be sure to write in your journals today while everything is fresh in your minds. By the time school begins, you'll already have a project under your belt in my class."

Jaris came to pick Chelsea up at Tubman at twelve fifteen. He was always good about picking her up and taking her places since she was grounded. Chelsea missed not being able to take the bus or ride her bike places. She hoped that when she became a freshman at Tubman, her parents would give her another chance. She missed her freedom. And she felt sorry for Jaris. He was generally good-natured but was a burden for him. But Chelsea felt bad that he was paying the price for her stupidity.

"Hi, Jaris," Chelsea greeted. "Thanks for picking me up."

"No problem, chili pepper," he responded.

"Jaris, you look kinda sad," Chelsea observed. "Wassup?"

"Just between us, Chelsea," Jaris confided, "Sereeta's mom had too much to drink last night. Me and Sereeta had to go downtown and pick her up."

"Ohhh," Chelsea groaned, "poor Sereeta!"

"Yeah, and that's not the worst part," Jaris added. "Some stupid neighbor kid at the Manley house saw us leading her up the walk. Now she's texting all her stupid friends about it. Everybody's gossiping. I'm afraid it'll get back to Sereeta and hurt her even more. Times like this, this instant communication stuff creeps me out. Before you even get home, some airhead is putting your private life out there for all to see."

"I'm sorry, Jaris," Chelsea sympathized. "You tell Sereeta we all love her a lot, and things are gonna get better. Tell her it doesn't matter what stupid people say."

CHAPTER SIX

Jaris was going to drop Chelsea off at home, then go to work at the Chicken Shack. As they neared the house, they saw Grandma Jessie's little red convertible in the driveway.

"Uh-oh, chili pepper," Jaris nodded toward the driveway. "Look who came to call. That can't be good news."

"Oh no!" Chelsea grumbled. "*Now* what's she gonna complain about? I hope it has nothing to do with my opossums."

Jessie Clymer was Mom's widowed mother, and Mom was very close to her. In fact, Mom was always on the phone with her, sharing all the details of the Spain family life. Grandma Jessie had never liked

Pop. When her daughter began dating Lorenzo Spain, she moved heaven and earth to try to break them up. Nothing worked. From time to time, she gently urged her daughter to end the marriage and find fulfillment with a man more suited to her. That kind of talk infuriated Chelsea and Jaris. To them, their grandmother was a meddling troublemaker, and they hated to see her coming.

Chelsea came in the front door, making a point of banging the door shut to express her displeasure with the visitor. "I'm home, Mom," she yelled. "Hi, Grandma."

"Oh, Chelsea," Grandma Jessie said in a warm voice, "Your mother's been telling me how you're working with vermin now. I do hope you've washed your hands well with antibacterial soap. If not, I have a bottle in my purse—"

Chelsea went into the living room. Her mother sat on a straight-backed chair, and her grandmother was reigning from the best over-stuffed chair in the room. That was the chair

that Pop usually sat in. Chelsea deeply re-
sented Grandma Jessie sitting in Pop's chair.
"I'm working with marsupials, Grandma, not
vermin," Chelsea replied bitterly. "Opossums, actually. They're very cute, and I thoroughly washed my hands before I left the
refuge. Shadrach made sure of that."

"Shadrach?" Grandma repeated the
name with clear distaste, glancing at her
daughter. "Now that would be the poor
disfigured man Chelsea is helping?"

Chelsea rolled her eyes. As usual, Mom
had told her mother everything, not leaving
out a single detail. Chelsea sent her mother
a dark look. Mom looked guiltily away,
concentrating on her lemonade and swish-
ing the ice cubes. They made lovely little
tinkling sounds.

"Shadrach is a war hero," Chelsea announced, not knowing whether he was or
not. "He got hurt in this war in Afghanistan,
I think. I'm not sure 'cause those war he-
roes don't like to talk about what they went
through. That's just the way they are."

"You really don't know how he became so severely scarred, do you, dear?" Grandma asked in a sickly sweet voice. "We don't want to be making up stories, do we? Has he told you about his condition?"

"One of the opossums told me," Chelsea snapped.

Mom looked up sharply. "Chelsea, don't be insolent," she scolded.

"I would imagine these creatures smell awful," Grandma remarked, shuddering. "Be sure to take a nice hot shower, dear. You don't want the stench sticking to you."

"I didn't notice any stench," Chelsea replied. She wanted to add "until I got in here," but didn't say it. She knew she'd be in really big trouble if she went that far.

"So, sweetheart," Grandma Jessie asked, "why do you want to save opossums? Isn't the city trying to get rid of them? I mean, they have programs to rid the city of all kinds of vermin—rats, gophers, squirrels, whatever. I think there's a vermin abatement program, and we pay our taxes into that. Yet you and this pathetic Shadrach character are trying to rescue them so that we are even more overrun with them. This neighborhood is already gravely afflicted with gangs and poverty and graffiti. Do we really need to encourage wild pests?"

Chelsea sat down in an uncomfortable rocker near her mother. She faced her grandmother, who was wriggling around to get more comfortable in Pop's chair. Chelsea felt she had no right to be sitting in that chair anyway. But Chelsea had another question to ask.

"Grandma," she began, "do you think we should wipe all the animals off the face of the earth? Who gave us the right to do that? Pastor Bromley said we got dominion over the earth, but we gotta protect it. I don't think we should kill all the little animals. Opossums aren't hurting anybody. They just want the chance to survive like everybody else."

Grandma Jessie didn't answer Chelsea. Instead, she turned and spoke to Mom in a distressed voice. "Monica, the poor child refers to the opossums as if they were people. Did you get that? They deserve to survive like *everybody* else. Did you hear that? Doesn't that alarm you?"

"Oh, Chelsea knows they're not people, Mom," Chelsea's mother responded with a nervous smile, taking a quick gulp of lemonade. "She just feels sorry for them."

"No," Chelsea insisted, wishing to cause trouble. "I do think they are sort of people. I think opossums should wear little coats and trousers, and maybe little top hats or beanies. Once they're educated, they could go to school too."

"Chelsea," Mom chided, "now you are being deliberately offensive."

"Should we kill all the songbirds too, Grandma," Chelsea asked. "Maybe we could spare the hummingbirds 'cause they're so tiny."

Again, Grandma Jessie ignored the girl. The woman finished her lemonade and said, "Monica, you have a problem. I am simply telling you that this child is going to give you grief. She is not even in senior high yet, and she is sarcastic and extremely rude. Not that this comes as any great surprise to me, with the father she has."

Chelsea realized she had gone too far. "I'm sorry, Grandma," she said. "It's just that the opossums are so cute, and they don't hurt anybody. It's fun to be helping them. I'm keeping a journal about working at the rescue center too. I'm gonna get credit in my science class at school when I start at Tubman. I'm already friends with the teacher, and we get along real good."

"Well, dear, just don't let one of those horrible things bite you," Grandma warned. "Rabies is no laughing matter, and everybody knows you can get rabies from those wild things."

"Not from opossums," Chelsea countered, digging into her backpack for the literature Shadrach gave her. "You can read it right here. Opossums can't get rabies 'cause of their low body temperature."

"Well, thank heaven for that," Grandma Jessie sighed. "But there must be all kinds of other nasty things they can transmit. I mean, they are so ugly and dirty looking."

The older woman cast a critical look in her daughter's direction. "I'm really surprised, Monica, that you let the child get involved in such filthy business. There are so many nice activities for young girls in the summer—dance lessons, music lessons, sewing . . ."

"I really like working with the opossums," Chelsea asserted.

Grandma Jessie took a final delicate sip of her lemonade. She then declared in an anguished voice, "Monica, the children are *so* like Lorenzo. It's simply amazing. I see so little of you in them, and so much of him." The loathing in her voice was only thinly veiled. "Speaking of your husband, how is the garage doing? I've been almost afraid to ask, knowing that your home hangs in the balance, hostage to this wild scheme of Lorenzo's."

"So far it seems to be going well, Mom," Monica Spain replied. "Of course, it hasn't been that long. But he has a lot of new business, and he's hired a young man to help him. The new mechanic seems very good."

"Mmm," Grandma Jessie sniffed. She almost seemed unhappy with the positive report. She looked at the beautiful gold watch on her wrist. "I must be going I'm afraid," she announced, "I am attending a board meeting at a children's charity I have recently taken an interest in. We are helping children appreciate the arts." She glanced at Chelsea and her daughter, "Of course that isn't as important as propagating vermin, but then what do I know? I'm from another generation. We used to set traps for vermin, but now we have refuges for them. Our priorities are vastly different."

As Grandma Jessie was about to leave, Chelsea said, "Bye, Grandma. I'd give you a hug, but . . . uh . . . you know, I've been with the opossums."

"Yes, that's considerate of you, dear. *And do shower*," Grandma Jessie instructed as she hurried for the door.

They heard her engine coming to life and the little red convertible backed out of the driveway. Mom turned to her daughter and said, "Stop laughing."

Chelsea was convulsed. She couldn't stop. Every time she tried to stop, she laughed harder.

"Chelsea Spain, stop!" Mom commanded. Then she covered her own mouth with her hand and started giggling. "Chelsea," she wailed, "look what you've done to me!"

The phone rang then. Mom answered it, and her face changed. She seemed troubled. "I'm so sorry to hear that," she said. "When was this? Oh dear. Well let's hope it all turned out all right. Let's just hope for the best, yes."

When she put down the phone, she frowned. "That was Nattie," Mom explained. "She thought I'd want to know that

Olivia Manley was drunk yesterday. So drunk that my son and his girlfriend had to practically carry her up the walk of her house. Nattie Harvey was, of course, enjoying every minute of telling me that. She is such a wicked gossip."

Mom sat down and for a moment put her face in her hands. Then she looked up, "Did you know about this, Chelsea?" she asked.

Chelsea didn't want her mother to be hurt. She couldn't admit that Jaris was confiding in his little sister but not his mother. So she said, "I heard it today. It's all over, Mom. Some kid who lives next door to Mrs. Manley is texting everybody. I guess it got to Nattie Harvey, and now she's making sure the whole world knows."

"Poor Sereeta," Mom moaned. "I don't know where this is going. Olivia Manley is like a runaway train. I shudder to think of the future for Sereeta. I worry about Jaris too. He's so involved in this, and it's so sad. I mean for a teenaged boy to have to bring his girl's intoxicated mother home at night. It's so awful."

"Maybe Sereeta's mom'll join some group," Chelsea suggested. "They help people, don't they?"

"Only if they want help," Mom responded sadly.

Much later, that evening, Chelsea went to her room to start her journal. She was so glad that Athena, Heston, and Maurice were with her. It made everything more fun and interesting. Besides, she was starting to build her little group of friends, as Jaris did. Chelsea really liked Heston. He wasn't really handsome or anything, but he was sweet and nice. And he liked Chelsea. She could tell.

Chelsea flopped on her bed and took her journal in hand. But she was too excited about her upcoming freshman year to write her entries.

A lot of the girls going into the freshman class at Tubman already had boyfriends. Now that Chelsea knew a boy who was sort of interested in her, she didn't feel so left out.

Chelsea turned again to her journal. After writing a while, she texted Athena. "My journal's going gr8t, Athena," Chelsea texted. "It was fun today, right? GTG."

Athena texted back right away. "Heston and me worked on our journals 2gether. He used my computer. He's 2 poor 2 go online. TTFN."

Chelsea was surprised and a little upset. Why didn't Heston come over and work on Chelsea's computer? What was he doing at Athena's house? Chelsea didn't live any farther from Heston than Athena did. What was the deal? Pop was nice to Heston when he came over here, so that wasn't a problem.

In her mind, Chelsea replayed the day at the opossum refuge. Had she said something that made Heston mad? Or did Heston just discover all of a sudden that he liked Athena more than he liked Chelsea? He and Athena did seem to be working together a lot. Maybe Heston was jealous that Chelsea and Maurice were talking a lot. Maybe Heston felt humiliated when he refused to hold the opossum and Maurice took Magic right away.

It was too early to go to sleep, but Chelsea lay there looking up at the ceiling. Why was she getting so upset over something this stupid, she wondered? Heston was just a friend. He wasn't a boyfriend, not yet anyway. Chelsea wasn't crazy about him or anything. But she thought it'd kind of cool if they'd hang together at Tubman, and she would feel good about it.

Now maybe he was Athena's boyfriend. Athena came to the opossum refuge wearing a real pretty tank top. Her jeans were so tight they looked like they were painted. Chelsea thought she was prettier than her anyway. Chelsea just wore a baggy old T-shirt and roomy jeans. Maybe Heston got caught up in how pretty Athena looked.

Chelsea called Heston on her cell phone. "Hi," she said, keeping her voice light and breezy. "I finished writing in my journal. You too?"

"Yeah," Heston replied. "I wanted to do a good job and get credit from Ms. Colbert."

"That's really nice of Ms. Colbert to give us credit and to be working with Shadrach like that," Chelsea remarked. "I think Athena had fun today too. Don't you think so, Heston?"

"I don't know," he answered.

Chelsea exchanged a few words with him, but she wasn't paying attention. She was thinking that he wasn't going to tell her about going to Athena's house and working with her on her computer. "If he didn't have a guilty conscience about it," she told herself, "he would've told me. He's got a crush on Athena! Pop was right. She's bad news. It's Athena's fault we all got in that Mercedes and rode at a hundred miles an hour with the Yates boys. It's Athena's fault I got busted. Now she's stolen Heston Crawford, who used to like me. I hate her so much. I'm not going to be her friend anymore."

Chelsea said a cold good-bye to Heston and slumped back on her bed.

"I don't need any friends!" Chelsea told herself bitterly. She stared at the ceiling again. She suddenly popped up and took her raggedy old teddy bear from the top of her bureau. She flopped back on the bed, hugged the teddy tightly, and felt about seven years old.

Chelsea knew Tubman was a big school, bigger than Marian Anderson Middle School. She dreaded that first day, walking onto that large campus and not knowing anybody. She depended on Athena, Keisha, and Inessa, but especially Athena. Athena—darn her!—was so much fun. Chelsea had relied on having her and Heston. It wouldn't be the same with just sour old Inessa and Keisha. Watching Athena and Heston slobbering over each other would just ruin everything for Chelsea.

Then Chelsea thought that Shadrach was smart. It was better to hang out with opossums rather than with people. Opossums weren't treacherous like people.

Chelsea heard Pop coming down the hall. As he usually did, he stuck his head through the doorway. "Bedtime pretty soon, little girl," he reminded her.

"Okay, Pop," Chelsea mumbled.

Pop's head disappeared, then reappeared.

Pop studied his daughter for a second and then came into the room.

"So," he asked, "what's with layin' here huggin' the old teddy bear? I thought we retired him. Somethin' bad happen today at the opossum place?"

"Oh no, Pop, it was great," Chelsea answered. "I loved it."

Pop came closer and sat on the edge of the bed. "Come on, baby. I see somethin' shiny on those cheeks. You been cryin'. Wassup, little girl?"

Chelsea picked at the teddy's worn ear. Then she spoke. "It's just . . . pretty soon I'll be going to Tubman, and it's such a big school. I don't know hardly anybody, and I'm scared I'll be all alone."

"You been lookin' forward to goin' to Tubman, Chelsea," Pop remarked. "What happened?"

"Well, Athena was my best friend, and I don't like her anymore," Chelsea explained. "She's hangin' with Heston Crawford now, who I *thought* liked me. That dirty rat of an Athena stole Heston at the opossum refuge. Pop, she's so sneaky. I didn't even see it happen. She was all dressed up in cool jeans. I guess Heston went crazy, 'cause now he's hangin' with her."

Pop sat there for a long moment without saying anything. Then he spoke to his daughter. "Lemme get this straight, little girl. So this is about a big romantic triangle? One person is my little fourteen-year-old girl, who has no business having a boyfriend anyway. Then there's this twit of an Athena Edson without a brain in her head. And finally the Romeo is that tall, gangly string bean dodo Heston Crawford.

Now he's hooked up with the airhead Athena. Is this what I'm hearing?"

"You make it all just sound stupid, Pop," Chelsea whined. "But I liked Heston, and I thought he liked me and I'm hurt."

"Heston Crawford is an idiot, little girl," Pop told her. "You will go to Tubman High School. By ten in the morning, you will have so many friends you won't know what to do with them. You will smile that big beautiful smile you got, and they'll gather around you like bees to a flower."

Pop reached over and took his daughter's hand in his. "Everybody loves you, Chelsea," he told her softly. "You don't have to worry about having friends. It's been that way all through school, little girl. It won't be no different at Tubman." Then his voice grew gruff, and he bulged his eyes for comic effect. "Your pop ever lie to you, baby?"

"No," Chelsea admitted.

"He ain't lying now either," Pop affirmed. He reached out and took his daughter in his arms in a big bear hug. Chelsea smelled all "his smells." His shaving lotion, a little whiff of oil from his pickup he fixed today, the gel he put on his beautiful black hair. A feeling of love and hope surged through her. She felt safe and happy.

"Want milk and a little something 'fore you get ready for bed?" Pop asked.

"No, Pop. I'm fine," she responded. "I'm feeling tired all of a sudden."

"Well, good," Pop said, "'cause it's time anyway. You have a good night's sleep, baby."

The father went down the hall, whistling.

Chelsea reread her work on her journal. She had planned to share what she'd written with Athena, and Athena had promised to do the same. They wanted to make sure they both had covered the main points and got all their facts straight. Now, of course, that wouldn't happen. Chelsea wasn't sure whom she'd miss most, Heston or Athena. She was pretty sure it would be Athena.

CHAPTER 7

Next Monday morning, the Spains were at the breakfast table.

"Oh look!" Pop exclaimed as he finished Monday's breakfast. He'd just finished popping a little sausage in his mouth. "I believe I see the airhead coming down the street on her bicycle. I sense a streak of bad luck comin' on. Aha, she's turnin' into our driveway, little girl. Here's Athena at the door . . ."

"Athena Edson has the nerve to come here?" Chelsea screeched loudly. Jaris almost dropped his spoon into his cornflakes. "What's goin' on?" The last time he heard, Chelsea and Athena were fast friends.

"Jaris, that dirty rat stole Heston Crawford from me at the opossum refuge,"

Chelsea explained. "He went to her house to work on the computer 'cause his family can't afford one. But he always came here and worked on *my* computer until that Athena stole him. She's so two-faced. She wore these really skinny jeans to the refuge. Heston like musta gone crazy. She made me look ugly in my old T-shirt and crummy big jeans. Ms. Colbert said we shouldn't wear anything nice, but Athena double-crossed me and dressed good, the rat. Now I've lost my best friend and my boyfriend."

"Man!" Jaris commented. "You go away for a few hours, and the whole world turns upside down while you're gone." He plunged another heaping spoonful of corn-flakes into his mouth.

Athena was pounding on the door. "Chelsea! Let me in! I see you in there!" she yelled.

"Hey, the whole neighborhood is wonderin' what's goin' on, little girl," Pop remarked. "We gotta let the airhead in. If we don't, old Mrs. Watley across the street is gonna imagine we got an emergency here. She might call the cops. Next thing you know, we got the ghetto birds overhead. So let's open the door. If you don't like what she has to say, you can pull her hair or somethin'."

Pop got up and went to the door. "Hey Athena, how's it going? You made any more trouble lately?" he asked.

Athena rushed past Pop and started babbling to Chelsea. "Chelsea, you can't imagine what that fool Heston did! He comes to my house at a really bad time. My parents were yelling and screaming at each other about who knows what—like I even care? He wants to use my computer. I go. 'You always use Chelsea's computer, so go there.' And he goes, 'I can't, 'cause she thinks I'm a wimp 'cause I wouldn't hold the opossum. Now I can't face her.' Girl, you gotta get that nerd off my back!"

"How you like that?" Pop asked, with a forkful of scrambled eggs loaded with catsup in his hand. He spoke to his daughter.

"Here you thought the dodo went for the skinny jeans." The eggs and catsup disappeared into Pop's mouth.

"*What*, Mr. Spain?" Athena asked.

"Nothin', nothin' at all," Pop replied. "I gotta get to the garage and help Boston fix those beaters. I can't stand the excitement around here."

Mom came from the kitchen with her buttered toast. "What is all the screaming in here about? . . . Oh, hello Athena, why are you screaming?" Mom asked.

"It's like real complicated, Monie," Pop explained. "Just eat your toast, and drink your coffee, and ignore all what's goin' on around here. We got romantic triangles and skinny jeans and airheads and dodos who are afraid of holding opossums. I must say, I would not be too keen on holding opossums myself since they seem to have big teeth."

Through all the commotion, Chelsea's gaze was riveted on Athena.

"You mean," Chelsea said slowly, "you and Heston aren't hanging out? I thought he went to your house to use the computer because he . . . you . . . I mean, you clicked or something."

"He came to my house 'cause he was ashamed he didn't hold that opossum," Athena told her. "You did, and he was scared. Now he's ashamed. You gotta talk to him. I don't want him at my house. He's weird. My parents are gonna be fighting a lot, too, 'cause Mom's big department store bills are coming in. I don't want visitors."

"Oh, Athena," Chelsea cried, hugging her friend. "You're my best friend in the whole world. I was so scared we weren't friends anymore!"

"Oh, this is beautiful!" Pop crowed. "Look at this. Our little girl is hugging the airhead. Is this beautiful, Jaris . . . Monie? You want to keep wonderful moments like this in your mind to think about when things are not goin' so good."

"Mr. Spain," Athena asked, "did you just call me an airhead?"

120

"Oh, that's like a pet name, Athena," Pop explained. "I use it for the really pretty girls. All that air you got in your head, makes you sparkle, Athena."

Athena's face was a little scrunched up, but the explanation seemed to be okay with her. Pop finished his last bite of eggs and toast and took a final swallow of coffee. Then he said, "Well, off to the beater factory."

He walked over to Mom and kissed her soundly on the lips. "Be good, baby," he directed. "Don't be lookin' at other guys, y'hear what I'm sayin'? I mean, a babe as beautiful as you, you're gonna have *them* lookin' at you. But don't you look back. After all, you're *my* beautiful airhead."

Pop winked at everybody and went out the door.

Mom was smiling despite herself. She announced, "The man is insane, of course, but the trouble is I'm in love with him. I'm in love with a madman."

Athena grabbed Chelsea's hand and said, "I've got tons of stuff to tell you.

121

Come on." She dragged Chelsea into Chelsea's bedroom, and they closed the door behind them.

Sitting on the edge of the bed, Chelsea asked, "Wassup, Athena?"

"Ms. Colbert has a daughter who's gonna be a freshman at Tubman too," Athena related. "Her name is Falisha. I met her at the Ice House, and she's really furious at her mom 'cause her mom has a boyfriend. I mean, not like a real boyfriend, but a guy she likes to hang with. Ms. Colbert's been divorced like forever. So it's been her and Falisha, and now Falisha doesn't want a stepfather. She's like ballistic about it."

"Wow!" Chelsea exclaimed. "Kinda like my brother's friend, Sereeta. It really bothered her when she was in middle school and her mom started going with this guy."

"No," Athena corrected her friend. "It's not just that Falisha doesn't want a stepfather. She hates this particular guy that her mom likes. The funny thing is, maybe Ms. Colbert isn't even gonna marry him or anything. But one time Falisha was looking out the window when he brought her mom home from some school thing, and they were kissing!"

Athena went on breathlessly, "Falisha said she was sick. She was so sick she almost upchucked. That's what she said."

"Is the guy a teacher at Tubman too?" Chelsea asked.

"He's kinda like a tutor and a maintenance man when they need something done," Athena said. "Girl, you are not gonna believe who the dude is. You are absolutely, totally not gonna believe it."

Chelsea grabbed Athena. "Tell me!" she cried.

"This is so wild, Chelsea! Ms. Colbert's friend is Shadrach!" Athena announced.

"No way!" Chelsea almost screamed. "It can't be true! Are you sure, Athena?"

"Falisha told me. She was all mad and everything," Athena affirmed. "She told me she hates Shadrach like totally. Y'hear what I'm sayin', girl? She hates the sight of him. She feels like Inessa does about how he looks. She says he's some kind of a monster."

"Athena," Chelsea almost whispered, "that's awesome news!"

Athena rattle on. "But Falisha's mom is so lonely, I guess. And her first husband, Falisha's father, was super mean to her. Then he just walked off, and she hasn't heard from him in years. She's only thirty-four years old, and she's probably so lonely. I bet she's like amazed at what a nice, gentle man Shadrach is. She'd probably given up believing there were guys in the world like him."

"Wow!" Chelsea gasped.

"And you know what else, Chelsea?" Athena added. "Falisha said her father used to hit her mom. He slapped Ms. Colbert around. Falisha was real little, but it scared her so much she hid in the closet. But all this is hush-hush, Chelsea. I'm only telling you 'cause you're my best friend and I know I can trust you. So it's just between us, 'kay?"

"You bet," Chelsea assured her friend.

"Oh, and one more thing, Chelsea," Athena went on. "Shadrach told Ms. Colbert and Falisha one day about how he got hurt. He hardly ever talks about it, but he wanted Ms. Colbert to know. Falisha just happened to hear it too."

"The war, huh?" Chelsea asked, leaning forward eagerly.

"Yeah," Athena replied. "It was one of those IEDs. I'm not sure what they are."

"I did a report on the Iraq war last year, Athena," Chelsea said. "'IED' stands for improvised explosive device. It's the way most of our soldiers got hurt. The guys they're fighting, they like put together all these different kinds of explosives with stuff they found. Then they put them on roads and stuff."

"We can't bring that up to Shadrach," Athena told her. "Falisha said he doesn't want to talk about it. His whole outfit got killed except for him, and he's got the guilts about it. I guess soldiers are like that sometimes when their buddies all die, and they make it. I guess they kinda feel bad that they made it and the others didn't."

Athena paused. "Falisha's nice," she remarked. "She can be a good friend for us. She fits right in with you and me and Keisha, and sorta with Inessa. She's not as much of a sorehead as Inessa. I mean, Ms. Colbert and Falisha just moved here a few months ago. Falisha doesn't know *anybody,* and she was so happy to meet me at the Ice House. I told her all about you guys, and I said she can hang with us. Oh Chel, you'll like her. She's into the kind of music we like too, sorta soft rock and alt."

"Wow, we already got a little gang going at Tubman," Chelsea squealed with delight. "It's like with my brother and this bunch he calls 'Alonee's posse.'"

"Yeah!" Athena affirmed. "When that creepy Kanika and Hana hassle us, we don't have to care. Chel, get Jaris to take you over to the Ice House today on his way to work. Falisha's mom is dropping her there. Heston and Maurice gonna be there too. We can go home with Maurice's mom. She's got a van. You think Jaris'll bring you?"

"Yeah, sure," Chelsea said.

"And please tell Heston," Athena begged, "that it's okay he didn't want to hold Magic. He got really freaked out that he looked like a coward in front of you. So maybe we'll see you about three, okay?"

"Yeah," Chelsea agreed. "Is it okay with Falisha if Keisha and Inessa know about Shadrach's army story?"

"Yeah, I told her we were all real close. The main thing there is we don't talk about it in front of Shadrach," Athena explained.

"Oh, Athena, I'm so excited about going to Tubman now," Chelsea chirped. "My brother and his friends got a special place where they all gather under the eucalyptus trees at lunchtime. We can pick a spot too, maybe under the pepper trees. That could be our spot, Athena."

Athena left and biked away. Chelsea nabbed Jaris before he left. "On your way to work, can you drop me off at the Ice House, Jaris? Somebody else is bringing me home," Chelsea asked.

"Sure," Jaris agreed. "I'm picking up Sereeta now, and we're gonna hang out for a while. I'll be home to get you around three, okay?"

"Super, Jare, you're cool," Chelsea told her brother.

Jaris picked up Sereeta at her grandmother's house. He was almost afraid to ask how her mother was, but he had to. It was like the elephant in the room that nobody wanted to talk about but that everyone knew was there. "Your mom doing okay, Sereeta?" he asked as they drove.

"Yeah," Sereeta answered. "She's got twitter now. She tweeted all her old friends. She found some girls she hadn't talked to in years on Facebook. She's going golfing with Perry. Mom hates golf, but she's trying to learn to like it for Perry's sake. I hope all of that, you know, occupies her time."

"It's hot today, babe," Jaris remarked. "Did you wear your swimsuit?"

Sereeta opened her button-down top, to reveal her pretty green swim suit.

"Great!" Jaris responded. "I feel like a little time at the beach, okay?"

"Yeah, sounds wonderful," Sereeta agreed. They had about four hours before Jaris had to go to work.

Jaris parked on the shoulder of the road, and they made their way down a narrow path to the sand. It was a weekday, so they had the beach pretty much to themselves. It was perfect.

"Did you ever build sand castles, Jaris?" Sereeta asked. She and Jaris joined hands and started walking slowly down the beach.

"Yeah I did," Jaris replied. "Nothing elaborate. One time I did manage to build a sand turtle. It looked pretty good. It's easy to build a sand turtle."

Sereeta laughed. "I built a really nice sand castle when I was about eleven," she recalled. "It had turrets and everything. The sand was just the right consistency. I'd brought along some of my little figures—princesses and princes. I put them on the sides of the castle. I remember it being a really bright day. We went and bought ice cream at a stand. I remember Mom and Dad splashing each other and laughing."

Sereeta turned suddenly and looked at Jaris. "You know, Jaris, you're really lucky with those parents of yours. I know they fight sometimes, but that's okay. They're there for you and Chelsea and for each other. Parents sometimes bug their kids for being so strict, and you want to be free to do what you like. But it's really good when your parents are strong and loving."

"I hear what you're saying, Sereeta," Jaris agreed.

They decided not swim. Instead, they just lay on the beach. Sereeta's dark green swimsuit made her look even more amazing than usual. She wore a green ribbon in her dark curly hair. She looked so beautiful, she took Jaris's breath away. She almost seemed unreal with her honey brown skin and the mass of glossy curls framing her face.

They put a towel on the sand, and Sereeta lay down. Jaris joined her, but not before giving her a peck on the cheek. They wiggled around for a second, getting comfortable on the towel.

After a moment or two, Sereeta recollected, "You loved me long before I loved you, Jaris. We were just kids in middle school, and you loved me."

"That's true," Jaris admitted. "All during those boring history classes with Mr. Finbar, I'd be looking at you and having fantasies."

"I always thought you were cute and nice, Jaris," Sereeta confided. "But I didn't care for you in *that* way until we were juniors at Tubman. Do you remember when I first told you that I loved you?"

"Yeah, I sure do," Jaris recalled right away. "It was after your birthday party. You'd gone for a ride with DeWayne who'd been drinking, and there was an accident. You were banged up pretty good. I had a birthday gift for you, and I gave it to you in the hospital. It was then you said you loved me."

"Those gold earrings." Sereeta remembered. "They're so precious to me now because they were your first gift to me. I told you that I loved you, Jaris. I told you that night and I meant it. But I didn't love you like I do now. It's so much more now. I can't imagine you not being in my life now. Whenever I'm sad or happy, or scared or excited, I think of you, and I feel your arms around me. Jaris, I was drowning so many times, and you rescued me."

"I couldn't make it without you, babe," Jaris told her.

They lay there, listening to the waves surging on the sand. Jaris took Sereeta's hand and kissed it. Then they took a last walk down the beach.

"That sand castle I built when I was eleven," Sereeta said. "The big waves came in and made short work of it. I lost all my little figures. I remember crying. I thought they'd drowned. My father scolded me for being silly. He said I was a big girl now. He said he'd go to the store and get me some new figures that would be even nicer. It was nothing to cry about."

Sereeta looked down as they walked in the sand. "But I wouldn't stop crying because I didn't want new figures. I'd had those figures since I was six or seven, and I *loved* them. I've thought about that silly event a lot, and I think that's how my father feels about people too. If something happens to the people around you, you can always find new people. My father has a nice new family now. I guess he's very happy even though he doesn't come to visit me. Everything can be replaced."

Sereeta stopped walking and faced Jaris. "But that's not true," she went on. "People can't be replaced. I don't know what would happen if you were ever out of my life, Jaris. I think I'd curl up and blow away like an old leaf when winter comes."

"That's never gonna happen," Jaris assured her, tightening his grip on her soft hand. "Just think, we're gonna be seniors soon, Sereeta. Mighty seniors, you and me."

Sereeta turned to him and laughed. Jaris couldn't remember ever feeling such happiness—such pure joy—as he felt now.

CHAPTER EIGHT

On his way to the Chicken Shack, Jaris dropped Chelsea off at the Ice House. Her friends were already there. She saw them around a table. There were Athena, Keisha, Inessa, Maurice, Heston, and a girl Chelsea had never seen before. It had to be Falisha.

Chelsea ordered a frozen strawberry yogurt and rushed over to the table. Athena said, "Chelsea, this is our new friend, Falisha."

"Hi, Falisha," Chelsea greeted. Falisha had cornrow hair, like Carissa, the girlfriend of one of Jaris's friends, Kevin. "I love your hair. I think it looks great," Chelsea commented.

Falisha wasn't pretty, but she was nice looking. She was one of these people who have nice features but who are put together in a way that isn't beautiful. Falisha was tall and thin, and she had pretty brown eyes. They were her best feature. They were smoky brown and full of mystery.

Chelsea could tell right away that Falisha was very shy. She would have trouble making friends. Chelsea was not like that. Even though she worried about not having friends, whenever she got among people, she talked to everybody. She could even be pushy. She remembered in first grade running around introducing herself to all the other kids. One girl in braids snorted, "Who's that pushy girl?"

But Falisha looked very nervous. Her smile was weak. It danced on and off her lips like a ballerina who wasn't sure of her routine. Only somebody as forceful as Athena could have bonded with her so quickly. Only Athena could have encouraged her to share her life story with all its secrets. Athena was so outgoing, she could overpower anyone's shyness and drag them into the group.

"You're not still mad at me that I didn't hold that opossum are you?" Heston asked Chelsea.

"I was never mad, silly," Chelsea replied, laughing. "I don't care if anybody wants to hold an opossum or not."

"*I* held old Magic right away," Maurice boasted. "I'm not afraid of nothin'."

"Yeah," Inessa remarked. "I see you riding your skateboard and flying through the air like a maniac. I'll tell you guys one thing. The day I touch an opossum or any other wild animal is the day you better have me locked up 'cause you know I just lost my mind."

"I *hate* opossums," Falisha announced in an emotional voice. "I think they're just so ugly I can't stand it." Chelsea figured Falisha wasn't just talking about opossums.

"One man's ugly is another man's beautiful," Keisha commented. "Everybody different. That's good. Otherwise we'd all like the same thing, and there wouldn't be enough of it to go around."

Athena turned to Falisha. "We gotta get something straight here, girl," she affirmed. "We're all friends, y'hear what I'm saying? Anything you say to us, stays with us. Me, Chelsea, Keisha, Inessa, Heston, and Maurice—we're here for each other. We got each other's backs, girl, y'hear me?"

Falisha smiled a little. "I never had real good friends before," she confided. "We kept moving a lot 'cause Mom was a substitute teacher. Now she's got a regular job."

"What I'm saying is," Athena explained, "we all talk from the heart. We don't have to be afraid. Like I'm admitting I'm dumb. Once, some guy gave me a sports bottle and said it was good stuff. I drank it and passed out 'cause it was whiskey. I was lying in the alley, and some old bum found me. Lucky for me, he called nine-one-one before something bad happened."

"Athena!" Falisha gasped, shocked. "Really?"

"Yeah, we're dumb sometimes," Athena admitted. "Like, 'nother time, me and Keisha and Chelsea got in a dude's car. He took us for a ride goin' over a hundred miles an hour. Chelsea and Keisha got grounded."

"I got busted for hanging with the Nite Ryders," Maurice added. "I don't do that no more."

Heston looked around nervously. He cleared his throat and confessed, "My thing is I get scared easy. I mean just seeing Chelsea's brother, Jaris, or her Pop, sends chills up my spine. I want to be real brave and stuff, like I'd of loved to pick up that old opossum and impress Chelsea. But I started gettin' shaky, and I hated myself."

"Hey dude," Maurice said, giving Heston a friendly poke in the shoulder, "seeing Chelsea's lunatic brother even scares me. Don't worry about it."

Falisha looked around at her new friends with a sense of wonder. Then she said, "I told Athena about my problem, and she asked if it was okay to tell you guys. I said okay. I didn't want it all around school, so kids won't make fun of me. See, my mom likes this guy Shadrach, the guy who rescues opossums. He has one eye, and he's scarred. He scares me, and I don't want him around. He gives me the creeps. I'm scared Mom'll marry him and he'll . . . you know, live in our house."

"Is it 'cause he looks bad that you don't like him, Falisha?" Chelsea asked.

"It's like everybody looks at him and shudders. I know he can't help it, but he creeps me out so bad," Falisha said.

"I don't blame you, Falisha," Inessa agreed. "He scares me too."

"I got this uncle," Maurice chimed in. "He so ugly, first time I seen him, I ran to my room and cried. I thought he was that weird critter that's supposed to live in the woods. Bigfoot. My uncle was huge and hairy. He's like got this shambling walk. Man, my flesh creeped. He got hairs coming outta his nose like six inches long . . . his ears too."

Keisha laughed hysterically. "Nobody got hairs six inches long coming out of their noses!" she howled.

"Ain't he ever hear of a hair clipper?" Heston asked.

"But then," Maurice went on, "he kept coming around. Next time I seen him, he wasn't so ugly. He offered to take me fishin' from the pier. I never been before, so I said okay. Now me and him go fishin' all the time, and he ain't bad lookin' no more."

"Yeah," Heston added. "The longer you know people, the more you kinda focus on their personality. Pretty soon, you don't even see the scars and stuff. Shadrach, he's such a good guy I don't notice the scars much."

"My older sister got zits last year, and I didn't even want to sit next to her in church," Keisha admitted.

"If I ever get bad zits, I'm gonna wear a mask," Chelsea swore.

"I know what you guys are doing," Falisha declared. "My grandmother always says, 'Beauty is what beauty does.' But I don't care what anybody says. I don't want that Shadrach near us. I hate those old opossums like nobody's business."

"Well," Inessa suggested, "your mom probably isn't even serious about the guy. He's probably just a friend."

Then Keisha added something. "My dad is getting too fat. He's got a big stomach. Mom and me are embarrassed by him. Mom nags him all the time to lose weight, but he loves his fried chicken. I'd rather have a skinny stepdad with a few scars than a big fat guy."

Keisha turned to Chelsea, "Your dad is sooo handsome, Chelsea.

Chelsea giggled. "Ewww, I gotta re-member to tell Pop that!" she snickered.

Falisha glanced out the window of the Ice House. "There's Mom. She's taking me home."

The group split up. Keisha and Inessa walked home. Heston had his bike. Chelsea and Athena and Maurice went with Ms. Colbert in her van.

Maurice's mom dropped Chelsea home, and Chelsea gave Falisha a good-bye hug. "I'm glad we're friends, Falisha," she told the girl. Falisha smiled, but she was stiff when Chelsea hugged her. She acted as though she wasn't used to getting hugs.

The following day, Jaris dropped Chelsea off at Tubman High. Chelsea wanted to show Ms. Colbert how she was coming along with her journal. Jaris would be back to pick her up. When Chelsea got to Ms. Colbert's office, the teacher was just walking into the classroom with Falisha. Falisha smiled at Chelsea and announced, "Mom, she's one of my new friends. I got a whole bunch of new friends now. We're all gonna eat together when we come to Tubman, and we're gonna study together and everything."

"I'm so happy Falisha is making nice new friends," Ms. Colbert said to Chelsea.

Chelsea looked at the teacher. She was really pretty, and she looked younger than her middle thirties. She had dark hair, dark eyes, and dark skin. Falisha was much lighter.

Chelsea felt sorry for Ms. Colbert. She was too young to live the rest of her life alone. And nice guys were hard to find, especially for women past thirty. That's what Chelsea heard on television, anyway. They said most of the good guys were already taken. Probably Ms. Colbert wanted a gentle man with a good heart who would take care of her and her daughter. Something about Shadrach had touched a chord in her heart. Chelsea thought it was too bad Falisha felt as she did about Shadrach.

Ms. Colbert glanced at Chelsea's journal and stated she was doing a good job so far. Then Ms. Colbert looked at Chelsea and asked, "Are you excited about coming to Tubman?"

"Yeah," Chelsea responded enthusiastically. "I liked Anderson Middle School, but

I really want to be here. I don't know yet what classes I'll have except for yours, Ms. Colbert. I'm glad I'll be in your class 'cause you're nice."

Ms. Colbert laughed. "Don't make any snap judgments, Chelsea. I'm a pretty tough grader. It's not easy getting an A out of me. Your older brother is a senior now at Tubman, isn't he?"

"Yeah, Jaris," Chelsea replied, wondering how Ms. Colbert already knew about Jaris. The teacher answered the question without Chelsea having to ask. "I've become friends with Torie McDowell since I came to work here. In fact, she helped me find this position. She and I were students together at UCLA. She was a senior when I was a junior. We belonged to the same sorority. Ms. McDowell has told me your brother is a fine student and a wonderful young man. He must be special to have impressed Ms. McDowell so much."

"I guess," Chelsea replied. She loved Jaris a lot, but he *was* only her brother. She saw him stumbling sleepily down the hall at home in his pajamas. She heard him singing in the shower and sounding pathetic. How could *her* brother be all that special? Maybe he was big shot Jaris Spain to the rest of the world. To Chelsea, he was often that overbearing guy.

Afterward, Ms. Colbert was leaving the school parking lot and found Chelsea standing alone.

"Chelsea," the teacher asked, "do you have ride home?"

"I don't know," Chelsea said. "My brother was supposed to pick me up, but he's not here yet. I tried calling him, but he's not answering."

"Come on, Chelsea," Ms. Colbert said. "Hop in. I can have you home in a few minutes."

Sitting in Ms. Colbert's van, Chelsea felt as though something was wrong.

In the Spain driveway, she jumped out of the van, thanked Ms. Colbert, and walked toward the front door. Everything

146

about the house looked the same. But nothing felt right.

When Chelsea went in the house, it was eerily quiet. Pop wasn't home from work yet, but Mom was supposed to be home. "Mom?" Chelsea called out, with a strange sense of foreboding.

"I'm in here," Mom called from her parent's bedroom. Mom didn't sound right, and Chelsea hurried to see her.

"You okay, Mom?" Chelsea asked. Her heart was pounding.

Mom was sitting in a chair next to the bed. "I have a splitting headache," she explained. "Something awful happened down at the garage."

"Is Pop okay?" Chelsea almost screamed.

"Yes, yes," Mom responded, holding her hand up for Chelsea to lower her voice. "He's down at the police station now with Jaris. He caught that kid he hired—that Boston Blake—stealing from the cash drawer. Your father confronted the kid, and

Boston pulled a knife." Mom was visibly shaken.

"Mommm," Chelsea cried, shaking now herself. "You sure Pop wasn't hurt? *You sure?*"

"He's all right," Mom answered, nodding. "He wrestled the knife from the kid. He got him down on the floor and got the knife away from him. It was so awful. Your father . . . your father could have been hurt or killed. He could have been stabbed by this kid. God only knows what might've happened. Your father is twice that kid's age. If he hadn't been able to overcome him, he'd probably have a knife sticking in his chest. He'd be in the ER with doctors fighting to save his life. Oh my God!" Mom's eyes filled with tears.

Chelsea put her arms around her mother and hugged her. "He's all right, isn't he? You're not keeping something from me, are you, Mom?" Chelsea begged to know.

"No, he's not hurt," Mom sighed. "I called Jaris, and he went down to the police station with your father. The police needed a statement about what happened."

"They arrested that Blake guy, huh?" Chelsea asked.

"Yes. When your father had him down, he called nine-one-one," Mom responded. "The police took him into custody. He was charged with robbery and attempted murder. Oh Chelsea, the police told your father that this guy's been in trouble before. He has a rap sheet. He's nineteen, and already he has a rap sheet. Your father hired him without checking anything. He said he had a certificate in auto repair from the community college, but your father didn't even check that. He just sealed the deal with a handshake. No references, nothing."

Mom sighed heavily. "Oh!" she continued. "Your father has this romantic idea that you just look into somebody's eyes. If you like what you see, you go with it." Anger was creeping into her voice, replacing the fear and shock she'd first felt.

"Poor Pop," Chelsea moaned. "I bet he feels terrible."

"*I* feel terrible too, Chelsea," Mom snapped bitterly. "We put a big mortgage on our home so that your father could own this garage. Now his first big decision has proved a disaster. It almost cost him his life. I'm still shaking just thinking about it. He goes and hires some criminal off the street. Mom was right. Your father has no sense. Nobody these days hires someone without checking their references, seeing if they have a criminal record."

"*Please,* Mom," Chelsea begged, "don't tell Grandma. She'll beat Pop over the head with this forever and ever. She'll never let him forget it."

"Maybe he should never forget it," Mom snapped. "Is that our biggest worry, that your father's feelings will be hurt? Heaven forbid that should happen. No, our big worry is that this is probably only the beginning of his rookie mistakes. In the end, they'll cost us not just the garage, but the roof over our heads!"

Pop's pickup, followed by Jaris's car, came into the driveway. Pop came in first. He had a bad bruise on his head, which he got falling against a desk while grappling with Boston Blake. Otherwise, he was unhurt. Mom rushed to him and hugged him. Chelsea threw her arms around her father and cried, "I'm so glad you're okay. *I was so scared!*"

"What a day!" Pop sighed deeply. "I thought this was a great kid. He knew his stuff, he was good with the customers. I watched him work. Not perfect, but definitely gettin' there. I went over the work he did, and it was great. I couldn't believe it. There he was in the office, helping himself to what was in the cash drawer. I go up behind him, and I say, 'Wassup, Boston?' He turns around, and he's lookin' wild. He's been stuffin' green ones in his pocket. I say, 'Hold on there. You ain't robbin' me, kid, not before I bust you in the chops.' He ain't havin' any of that. Next thing I know, he's got his knife out. He's gonna kill me, I'm thinkin', so I go after him."

The perspiration was still glistening on Pop's brow. "We went at each other for a coupla minutes, and I got him down. I called nine-one-one, and they were there real quick."

Pop shook his head. "I trusted this kid. I really liked him. What a lousy little bum."

"Lorenzo," Mom stated, "you didn't do a background check on Boston Blake." Her voice was stern. "You didn't follow the first rule when hiring people. You didn't do a security check. You gave him access to your office and your business, and you didn't know him from Adam."

Pop stood there, his eyes narrowing. He spoke darkly to his wife. "I ain't had a bad enough day. I almost got a blade stuck in my chest. I banged my head on the desk. Now I got to be scolded by this lady who should be my loving, supportive wife?" Anger darkened his eyes.

"Lorenzo, don't be a child!" Mom cried. "You made a terrible mistake. You failed to check out this man. That mistake could have cost you your life and destroyed this family! What other stupid mistakes are you making? I'd just like to know that. Do you realize what you've put me through today?"

"I don't need this," Pop huffed. He turned and went back outside.

Jaris ran after him. "Pop, don't mind Mom. She's just hysterical. She doesn't know what she's saying. Come back inside, Pop," Jaris pleaded. "Take a nice hot shower and rest."

Pop shoved Jaris out of his way and climbed into the cab of the pickup truck. He backed it out the driveway and went roaring down the street like a maniac. Jaris came back inside the house, his face a mask of anguish. He looked at his mother. "Mom, couldn't you have just held the lecture till the guy got his breath?" he asked. "He almost died today. He fought a man half his

153

age who mighta killed him. Couldn't you cut him some slack?"

Mom's eyes filled with rage. "Your father put this whole family at risk. He bought that stupid garage when he didn't know what he was doing. Now he hires a dangerous criminal to work in the garage, and the guy almost kills him. But it's *my* fault! Oh yes, my bad! I should clap my hands and say, 'Good job, Lorenzo!'"

Jaris felt that maybe he could have held off the lecture too. "Only a fool neglects to check out his employees," Mom went on. "I'm sick and tired of your father messing up and you kids making me the villain. I am sick and tired of it!"

Mom stomped down the hall, entered the bedroom, and slammed the door behind her. Jaris and Chelsea heard her loud sobbing soon after, and it continued for a long time.

"Jaris?" Chelsea whimpered, "It's gonna be okay, isn't it?"

Jaris didn't answer for a few seconds. He didn't know the answer to Chelsea's question. But the terrified look in Chelsea's big eyes forced him to make up something. "Yeah, sure," he answered halfheartedly. "Was an awful thing that happened. They're both . . . uh . . . not thinking straight. They'll cool down. It'll be okay, chili pepper."

CHAPTER NINE

The illuminated face of Jaris's alarm clock glared at him in the darkness. It was ten thirty. Even in the bad old days, when Pop sometimes stopped at a bar after work, he came in before now. Jaris had showered and put on his pajamas, but he couldn't sleep. He couldn't even think about sleeping. His eyes were wide and staring. He checked the clock every minute.

Jaris's imagination ran wild. Maybe this was all just too much for his father. Maybe Pop had started drinking again. Some time ago, he had taken the pledge at Pastor Bromley's church, and he hadn't had a drop since then. Not in months. But maybe today he broke the pledge. Maybe he'd been drinking, and a cop stopped him on his way home. Maybe now he had a DUI on top of everything else. Or maybe he'd been in an accident. He was in a terrible mood when he drove off. Maybe he came to some intersection and didn't notice the red light until he heard the crash.

Jaris had stopped twice at the garage while Boston Blake worked there. He seemed like a nice young guy with a broad smile. He had big shoulders, and Jaris thought he probably played football in high school. Jaris knew his father should have done a background check. Mom was right. But Pop was impressed with the friendly, polite, smooth talking young man. And Blake did know his way around engines. It all made sense. Blake had finished his course at the community college, and now Pop was giving him his first break. Pop was pleased to be doing that—to be giving a nice kid a hand up.

Then Jaris heard Pop's pickup in the driveway. The boy sat bolt upright in bed. It was almost eleven. Jaris froze. At least Pop made it home. That was a good thing. Jaris listened for the sound of him coming in, his footfall. When he'd been drinking, he sounded a little wobbly. But tonight he sounded okay.

Pop came down the hall. Pretty soon, Jaris heard the hot water running for a shower. Jaris listened for the tap to go off. In the past, when there was trouble, Pop slept on the couch in the living room. But this time he seemed to be going for his parents' bedroom, which was right next to Jaris's.

Jaris tensed up, wondering if the fighting would resume. He heard his mother's voice first. "I'm sorry, Lorenzo. I shouldn't have—" she began.

"I'm sorry too, babe. I made a bone-headed mistake. I just didn't want to be reminded of it," Pop replied.

"I'm so glad you're okay, Lorenzo. I couldn't make it w-without you," Mom said softly, her voice breaking.

There was silence then. He smiled and went to sleep.

The next Saturday, Chelsea, Athena, Maurice, and Heston again went to the opossum rescue center in Ms. Colbert's van. This time, everybody knew what to do. The four teenagers accomplished a lot. They replaced the soiled newspapers in the cages, cleaned up the bin where the opossum babies lived, and put out fresh food and water. Toward the end of the session, Ms. Colbert returned in the van.

"Everything looks good, Shadrach," she commented, looking around. "Smells nice and fresh too."

"The kids were great," Shadrach responded. "I'm glad you're here too, 'cause we were thinking about releasing Magic tonight. If anybody is free and wants to see it happen, well, now's the time to speak up."

"Oh, I'd love to see Magic go back in the wild," Chelsea cried.

"Me too," Athena echoed. "Anything to get me out of my house."

Maurice and Heston wanted to come too. So Ms. Colbert suggested, "I'll pick you guys up at your houses. Then we'll come here and follow Shadrach to wherever he sees a good release spot."

"That's so nice of you, Ms. Colbert," Chelsea remarked.

"It's no problem," Ms. Colbert said. "You guys all live near each other. So, about eight-thirty good, Shadrach?"

"Yeah, fine," he answered. "We should be finished by nine, nine-thirty. I've got several spots in mind. We gotta pick just the right one. A brushy area at the edge of a neighborhood. The poorer the neighborhood, the better 'cause those folks tend to be more tolerant of wild things. They won't mind an opossum occasionally eating off their cat food. Now the richer folks prefer stone animals in their yards . . . stone lions, maybe a stone chipmunk, or two."

"Will ol' Magic run like a deer when you release him?" Heston asked.

Shadrach laughed. "Opossums kinda ramble, Heston," he responded. "They can't run like deer. That's why so many of them get hit in the street. They can't get out of the way fast enough. But watch when Magic gets it into his head that he's free, that he's back in the wild kingdom. He's gonna ramble real fast, you better believe it. They just explode with joy."

Shadrach glanced lovingly over at Magic. "I'm telling you guys," he continued, "this is the best part of the whole deal. This is what makes all the hard work worthwhile. This is the night I'm thinking about when I'm dealing with all that wet newspaper. Magic came here all skinny and bloody, and he didn't have a future. We rescued him and tonight it pays off. He's young. He'll do fine. He'll find himself a girl opossum, and pretty soon his babies're resting in her pouch."

As Ms. Colbert handed everyone permission slips to sign, Chelsea watched Shadrach. He looked happier than Chelsea had ever seen him.

When Chelsea got home, she told her mother about the planned release of Magic. "Ms. Colbert, our science teacher is gonna pick us up about eight-thirty. We're following Shadrach to a good place where he'll free Magic."

"Well," Mom agreed, "as long as your teacher is with you. But be careful out there in the woods."

"Heston and Maurice are coming too, Mom," Chelsea chirped. "It's gonna be so fun." Then she hesitated. "Uh . . . Mom," she asked, "is Pop doing okay at the garage by himself?"

"Yes," Mom answered. "Mr. Jackson has come by to help. All those years your father bad-mouthed him, and now he turns out to be a friend. He doesn't need the money, but he knows your dad needs help until he can find another mechanic. So Jackson is fixing cars alongside your dad.

Three young guys have already put in applications, and this time your father is checking them out."

Mom looked pointedly at Chelsea. "And just for your information, young lady, I never told Grandma anything about what happened."

Chelsea gave her mother a big hug. "Thanks, Mom!"

The other three teens were already in the car as Ms. Colbert pulled up to the Spain house. Clutching her journal, Chelsea ran out to join them. They drove the short distance to Indigo Street and began following Shadrach's truck. Magic was already in a pet carrier in the truck.

"I bet Magic wonders what's happening," Chelsea commented.

"Oh, Chelsea," Athena laughed, "opossums don't wonder about stuff."

The moon was a crescent, but there was enough light to see.

"Have you ever seen a release before?" Heston asked Ms. Colbert.

"One time. It was really cool," she answered. "Up until then, I never really saw the value in rescuing the poor little critters just to live in cages. But suddenly it all made sense." Ms. Colbert smiled and remarked, "Shad knows what he's doing."

Chelsea's ears perked up. Ms. Colbert called Shadrach "Shad" in a warm and friendly way. Maybe Falisha really did have something to worry about.

"He's slowing down," Ms. Colbert noted. "This looks like a good area. Yeah, he's pulling over."

She drove in behind him and parked. Everybody got out. "Now we need to be very quiet, you guys," the teacher instructed. "Magic has been through a lot. We need to let him hear the sounds of the brush, not our voices."

Shadrach lifted the carrier from the truck and took it a short distance into the brush. The others followed single file.

"Smell the air around here," Shadrach whispered. "Smells damp. There's a little stream over there. Even when there's not a lotta rain, runoff from people sprinkling their yards drains in."

Ms. Colbert and the four teenagers followed Shadrach as he walked deeper into the brush. "Don't want to let him out in an unsafe place," Shadrach whispered.

The teacher and students stood silently, listening in awe. Chelsea thought, "Shadrach is right. This is wonderful and exciting." They all moved off a little deeper into the brush.

Suddenly Shadrach stopped. He set the carrier on the ground. He was so intent on what he was doing that he seemed oblivious to the teenagers and Ms. Colbert. Shadrach then spoke to Magic in a somber voice. "Okay, Magic, this is it, the parting of the ways, buddy. Don't go running in the street now, hear? Plenty nice crickets and cockroaches to eat around here, y'hear what I'm saying? Hear those crickets chirping away?"

Shadrach knelt on the ground and opened the door of the carrier. He pulled some apple slices in his pocket and tossed them on the ground in front of the open door. Magic crawled from the carrier. He sniffed an apple slice. He scarfed them all up. Then he vanished in a silvery blur, shambling as fast as he could.

Shadrach stood up and laughed. In the darkness, you couldn't see his scarred face. He looked like a tall, handsome man laughing heartily. "Ain't he just like a kid?" Shadrach noted with mock hurt. "You bust your butt getting them hale and hearty. Then the first chance they get, they leave you in their dust. Not even a backward glance. *Adios*, Magic. Have a blast."

"That was awesome!" Chelsea gasped, still in a hushed tone. There was something unreal, even spiritual about the moment. They had done a very good thing for a little creature who had no way of repaying the kindness. That made the release even more wonderful.

"You think you'll ever see Magic again, Shadrach?" Maurice asked.

"I hope not," Shadrach answered emphatically. "If I see him again, it means he's in trouble. But I think he'll be okay."

Ms. Colbert walked the students back to the street. She made sure everyone was in the van. Then she said, "I'm going to help Shad with the carrier. I'll be right back. On the way home, we'll stop at the Ice House for cones."

Chelsea wondered why Shadrach couldn't get the carrier on his truck by himself. Why would he need Ms. Colbert's help? The others were thinking the same thing and grinning.

They all unbuckled their seat belts and pushed forward to peer through the windshield. Mrs. Colbert and Shadrach were standing in front of the pickup. The truck was between them and the van. Even so, the students could just about see through the rear window of the truck. The two figures came together.

"He kissed her!" Maurice crowed in a low tone. "The dude kissed the teacher!"

"Don't tell Falisha," Athena said, "she'll freak."

"Why shouldn't she be happy her mom found a nice guy?" Maurice asked.

"'Cause Shadrach turns her off," Athena explained.

"Big deal!" Maurice responded. "My whole family turns me off, but I don't mess with what they want to do. I don't mess with them, and they don't mess with me."

"What's that mean, Maurice?" Chelsea asked.

"Means my folks don't pay much attention to me," Maurice replied. "Us kids kinda raise ourselves. It's okay."

"My parents are sort like that too," Athena added. "They got so much stuff going in their lives that sometimes they forget I even exist."

"My parents are on my case twenty-four-seven," Heston remarked.

"Mine too," Chelsea said.

"And then you got that lunatic brother watching over you too," Maurice told her, shuddering.

Mrs. Colbert started back to the van. The students scrambled back into their seats and buckled up.

When Ms. Colbert got into the driver's seat, she seemed in a very good mood. "That was special, wasn't it, you guys?" she commented.

"Yeah," Chelsea agreed. "Magic took off and never looked back. He had food and water and safety in that little cage back at the shelter. But he didn't have what he really wanted—freedom. He's got that now."

"Freedom's a great thing," Athena remarked. "But there was a girl rock-and-roll singer a long time ago. Mom liked her. I think her name was Janis something. Anyhow, she was big in Mom's time. She had this line in a song of hers. Freedom is sorta just another way of saying nothing left to lose, or something like that."

The other kids were staring at Athena. They weren't sure where she was going with this. "I guess it's not that way with opossums," Athena continued, "but for people. I mean, what if you can do anything you want without even telling anybody? Does that mean you're really, really free? Or does it mean nobody cares much about you?"

Chelsea looked at Athena and felt bad. Chelsea knew Athena's parents weren't like Mom and Pop. Chelsea's parents went a little crazy when she went on that dangerous car ride with the Yates brothers. But not Athena's mom and dad. They didn't seem very concerned. Chelsea always thought their reaction didn't matter to Athena. But maybe it did.

They stopped for yogurt cones, and Ms. Colbert dropped Chelsea home at ten. Mom and Pop were in the living room, discussing which new mechanic Pop should hire.

Mom looked up when Chelsea appeared. "Have fun tonight sweetie?" she asked.

"Oh yeah, Mom, it was great," Chelsea responded. "Magic is free now, and it was beautiful. Hi, Pop. You decided who to hire yet?"

"No, little girl," Pop answered with a half smile on his face. "Your Mom wants to make the decision. She's got me on a short leash now."

"Oh, Lorenzo," Mom laughed. "Don't be silly."

"Oh yeah," Pop insisted. "She's wantin' to be assistant manager of the beater shop now. Wantin' to make sure the old man don't screw up no more." Pop sounded sarcastic, but not in an angry way. He was, as usual, poking fun at Mom.

"Oh, Lorenzo," Mom corrected him, "it's just that I know two of the boys you're considering. I think I can give you some valuable input. They're both good boys. And they're probably good mechanics if they graduated from the community college with auto repair certificates. Now Rashard Jefferson is a nice quiet boy, very

171

trustworthy. But Darnell Meredith is not only that, but he has a great personality. Your customers would really like him. He's really sharp too. He was making money doing oil changes for people in the neighborhood when he was at Anderson Middle School."

"Well, Madame Chairwoman, you make the call," Pop announced. "You tell me who to hire, and it's done."

Mom laughed again. She was clearly enjoying the fact that Pop was asking for her opinion. "Stop being silly, Lorenzo. You couldn't go wrong with either boy. But if I were you, I'd hire Darnell."

"I'll call 'im Monday mornin'," Pop declared.

Later, Pop was walking behind Chelsea as she went to her room. "So the little opossum got his send-off tonight, huh, little girl?" he asked.

"Yeah," Chelsea responded, a little sleepily. She stopped and turned to face her father. "Shadrach released Magic. It was kinda sad to see him go, but it was great. I got so much good stuff in my journal about working at the rescue place. I'm way ahead of most of the freshman 'cause I already know and like one of my teachers."

Chelsea then paused. "Pop, will you have to . . . you know, go to court against that guy who tried to rob you?"

"I guess so," Pop said.

"He didn't belong to a gang or anything, did he, Pop?" Chelsea asked. She dreaded the thought of Boston Blake's fellow gang members coming after Pop.

"Not sure, baby," Pop replied. "But he had no tattoos, didn't dress funny. 'Sides, why would he be workin' in a fix-it shop if he was in a gang?"

"Still it kinda scares me that . . . you know, he'll be mad at you and stuff for sending him to jail," Chelsea told her father.

"I'm not thrilled about it either, little girl," Pop admitted. "But the kid has got to be stopped before he does something real bad. I can't let fear stop me from telling the truth about what happened."

"But what if he has bad friends and—" Chelsea started to say.

"Baby, you can't think about stuff like that," Pop cut in. "The kid pulled a knife. That's bad. He needs to spend some time in the slammer. Maybe then he'll straighten out and be okay. But I gotta do my duty. A man ain't much of a man if he lets fear get the best of him."

Pop realized that speech wasn't what Chelsea was worried about. "But don't worry about it, little girl," he changed his tack. "The kid probably has a lawyer. He'll work out some plea bargain so there won't even be a trial. Don't worry about it. You got more important things to think about, okay?" Pop gave Chelsea a hug, and she went into her room.

Lying on her bed, Chelsea checked over her journal. She couldn't believe all she had written. Shadrach's work had really touched her. Working with the injured and sick opossums and the babies had helped Chelsea make her decision. Someday she might be a veterinarian.

After she fell asleep that night, she even dreamed about opossums. In her dream, Magic reclaimed his place in the wild kingdom to much fanfare. All his old friends welcomed him back.

CHAPTER TEN

The next day, Jaris wanted to take Sereeta to the Ice House for a frozen yogurt. He asked Chelsea if she wanted to tag along. It was a hot day, and Chelsea jumped at the chance of eating something icy. All the way down the road, she struggled to decide what flavor she would choose for this unexpected treat.

Then, by the side of the road, Chelsea saw something bloody.

"Jaris!" she screamed. "A car killed another opossum!"

Sereeta got a sad look on her face. "The poor thing. I hope it didn't suffer," she remarked.

"Jaris," Chelsea said, "maybe it's a mother opossum, and she still has babies in her pouch. Shadrach says that sometimes happens. Then the poor babies just die slowly by the roadside. Could we stop and take a quick look?"

Jaris looked unhappy at the suggestion. "Uh, I think it's just a male opossum, Chelsea," he responded. "And he's dead, so he's not suffering."

"How do you know?" Chelsea demanded. "Couldn't you stop for just a minute so I could make sure?"

"Let's stop, Jaris," Sereeta urged. "Now I'm worried too. I'll keep thinking about it if we don't stop. I'll be thinking those little opossum babies are dying in the heat. Chelsea and I'll just jump out of the car and look."

By this time, the car had passed the dead opossum. Jaris made a U-turn and pulled to the side of the road near the dead opossum. Sereeta and Chelsea hurried over to the animal. Chelsea got there first. The adult opossum was bleeding from the head where the car had struck it.

There was no more life in the adult opossum, but it was a female. The half exposed pouch was filled with tiny, squirming babies.

"Jaris!" Chelsea screamed. "She has babies, and they're still alive!"

Jaris got out of the car as Chelsea was pulling an old towel from the trunk. "We can wrap them in this," Chelsea directed. "Shadrach told me just how to pick them up without hurting them."

"*What?*" Jaris groaned. "Chelsea, they're so tiny. They can't ever live outside the mother. Chili pepper, be reasonable. You can't save them."

"So what should we do?" Chelsea demanded, now in tears. "Just leave them to slowly die out here in the sun?" Chelsea was shaking with emotion.

"That guy Shadrach," Sereeta asked, "he's near here isn't he? On Indigo Street?

I've passed his place on my bike. We could just take them there. It wouldn't take long."

Sereeta helped Chelsea load the dead mother opossum along with her pouch of babies into the towel. They had made a kind of sack from the towel. Sereeta and Chelsea sat in the back seat of Jaris's Honda, both holding a corner of the sack. Jaris had a look of total bewilderment on his face as he drove toward the refuge.

"His pickup is there in the yard," Chelsea pointed. "Shadrach's home! He'll help us now."

Shadrach answered Chelsea's knock immediately. "Oh, hi Chel," he began to say.

"Oh, Shadrach," Chelsea began to rattle, "we found a dead mother opossum by the side of the road where a car hit her. She's got lotsa live babies in her pouch, and I know you can save them. We put the mother and babies in a towel, and I'm sure you can save the babies. I just know it. Will you help, Shadrach?"

"Sure!" he agreed, following Chelsea to the car. He lifted the towel sack up and took it inside. After a few moments, he shook his head. "I'm sorry, Chelsea, but they're just too young to be saved," he told her sadly.

"Oh, but they're alive," Chelsea protested. "You can—"

"No, Chelsea, look how pink they are, like little worms," Shadrach pointed out.

Chelsea was so sure Shadrach could save the baby opossums. She looked at them, and tears ran down her face.

"They'd only suffer if we let them live any longer," Shadrach advised. "There's a veterinarian over on Hockins Street, just around the corner. He helps me with the opossums. I'll take them over right away, and they'll be put down."

Shadrach studied Chelsea closely, and he said gently, "I'm sorry, Chelsea. I know you wanted a different outcome. You don't have to come with me to the vet. You did a good thing bringing the little critters in.

You've spared them a lot of suffering out there on the road."

"I want to go with you to the vet," Chelsea insisted.

Shadrach looked at Jaris and Sereeta. They nodded.

"We'll follow you over," Jaris said.

The veterinarian was an elderly man who seemed very kind. He examined the baby opossums and declared, "They can't survive at this stage. They'd just die slowly."

Shadrach said, "This little girl found the dead mother and the babies on the side of the road. I told her we couldn't save them."

The veterinarian looked at Chelsea and smiled. "You have a good heart, child." Then he disappeared into another room with the baby opossums.

Chelsea stood there, wiping away her tears. "I so hoped they could be saved. They were like moving around," she sobbed. "I could feel them moving under the towel. I was so happy they were alive."

Shadrach put his hand on Chelsea's shoulder. "They would have died slowly in that pouch on the road, Chelsea. They would have suffered. You saved them from that. You rescued them from needless pain. You spared helpless little critters a lot of suffering. That's a beautiful thing. You can be proud of that."

Jaris, Sereeta, and Chelsea were finally back in the car on the way to the Ice House.

"You're one special kid, Chelsea," Sereeta commented.

"Anybody woulda felt sorry for those poor little things," Chelsea responded.

"But not anybody would have done something about it, Chelsea," Sereeta said. "That's what makes *you* special."

In a little while, they were sitting in the Ice House and eating frozen yogurt. Jasmine Benson and two of her friends came in and sat nearby. The other two girls with Jasmine were from Lincoln High. Jasmine was talking in a loud voice that almost anybody in the yogurt shop could hear. She was so busy laughing and talking, she had not noticed Jaris and Sereeta.

"She was really drunk, and her daughter and her boyfriend had to practically carry her into the house," Jasmine crowed. "One time too, she came to Tubman High really drunk, and the teachers had to take her home and—" At that moment, Jasmine saw Sereeta and dropped her voice to a whisper. She said something to the two Lincoln High girls, and they looked over at Sereeta.

Jaris felt sick at the pain on Sereeta's face. He thought this is how it's going to be during Sereeta's senior year at Tubman. Girls like Jasmine gossiping about Sereeta's mother and her alcohol problems. Mean girls like Jasmine who loved to gossip about other people no matter how much they hurt people.

Maybe the worst part was that Jasmine would never admit that she reveled in the failures of other people. She would simply say that she was talking about it because she felt so *sorry* for Sereeta. She wanted to share that sorrow with other girls. Jasmine would say that she was just pointing out to those other girls how brave Sereeta was. After all, she was continuing to come to school, even though her mother was a laughingstock.

Jaris would have liked to go over to Jasmine's table and spill the rest of his soda over her head. But that would have just hurt Sereeta even more.

"I guess we're all done here," Jaris remarked, as Chelsea took the last spoonful of her yogurt. On their way out, Jaris gave Jasmine the dirtiest look he could muster. When Jasmine saw Jaris, she started to smile and greet him. Then she realized he'd heard everything. She saw the hatred in his eyes, and she said nothing.

Jaris thought about telling Sereeta how sorry he was, but doing that didn't make sense either. She knew he was sorry. Some people in the world were creepy, like Jasmine, but what good would talking about it do?

During the car ride home, Jaris had made a good bit of money this week, much of it in tips from the Chicken Shack. He had already added to his small savings account. He had also been planning to donate some money to a charity. In fact, he had the cash on him. He'd expected to over to the church this afternoon.

Now he posed a question to Chelsea. "That guy Shadrach, he takes care of the opossums with just his own money and some donations, right?"

"Yeah," Chelsea replied.

"I got a little money to give," Jaris told her. "I'll give half to Pastor Bromley's program for the foster kids and half to Shadrach. I'll give you the money for Shadrach, and you can give it to him the next time you see him."

Chelsea grinned broadly, "Oh, that's great, Jaris. How about if we go together and give it to him?"

"Okay, it's not too late," Jaris agreed.

They doubled back to the opossum rescue center and knocked on the door. When Shadrach appeared, Chelsea made the announcement. "My brother thinks you're a great guy, Shadrach. He wants to make a donation to help you with the opossums."

Jaris peeled off two twenties and a ten and handed it to Shadrach.

"Hey, thanks a lot!" Shadrach responded. "You guys want to come in? I live in a small apartment next to the shelter. I got some nice cold sodas."

"Yeah, sure," Jaris agreed.

They entered a tiny apartment with a single bedroom, living room, and kitchen. Shadrach pulled sodas from the refrigerator, and the three teenagers sat at the kitchen table. "You been hanging here for long, Shadrach?" Jaris asked.

"Oh, maybe two years," he answered.

"How come you like opossums so much?" Sereeta asked. "I think they're kinda cute, but not everybody does."

Shadrach laughed. "That's putting it mildly. If there was an ugly contest among the animals, opossums would come in first," he chuckled. "Maybe that's what attracted me to them. People like foxes, raccoons, even chipmunks. But the poor opossum is right there next to rats."

Sereeta sipped her soda and made a comment. "I bet you like all kinds of animals, people too. You can tell when somebody has compassion."

"That's a nice compliment," Shadrach replied, "but probably half true. I do like all animals, but people . . . not so much I'm afraid."

Chelsea had always noticed a deep loneliness in Shadrach's face. It wasn't just the scarring in his cheek, but an overall emptiness and sadness. That's why Chelsea was so happy when Ms. Colbert kissed him.

"I don't want to be nosy," Jaris asked. "But your injury looks like it mighta from an IED."

"Yep!" Shadrach answered. "Being in a war kinda can sour you on humanity sometimes. You wonder why such stuff happens. Like no opossum ever planted a roadside bomb, y'hear what I'm saying?"

It was an uneasy moment of silence. Jaris responded, "I hear ya, man."

Shadrach broke the silence then. "I'm doing better now. Things are looking up." He talked a little about his background. He'd been bitter and lonely for a long time. He drifted around the country, taking various jobs. He was a college graduate with a degree in mathematics. He wanted to use that, but he wasn't ready for steady work.

Then he talked about a turnaround event in his life. One day, Jaris was driving Chelsea and the other girls to the mall. They saw Shadrach at the side of the road with that wounded opossum. Everything changed that day for Shadrach. Nobody had cracked Shadrach's wall of isolation quite like Chelsea Spain had. She had come bounding into his life like a half-pint tornado. She was a beautiful, bubbly little girl who seemed totally accepting of the way he looked.

Shadrach had looked into the eyes of dozens of people since he was wounded. He always saw a lot of shock, even horror, or at least discomfort.

But Chelsea looked right at him. All she saw was a man holding a hurt animal, and she was worried about its fate. In an eye blink, she lifted Shadrach's spirits as they had not been lifted in a long time. If a pretty little girl like her could look at him and not be put off, well then maybe he wasn't so bad-looking at all. Maybe a lot of the shock he thought he saw was in his mind. In a strange way, Chelsea had rescued him that day while he was rescuing the opossum.

Chelsea didn't know what to say, and so she said nothing.

Shadrach smiled at her. He seemed to want to talk about things he hadn't talked about in years. These three teenagers called to something deep within him, something that had been locked up for a long time.

"I was engaged to be married when I was deployed to Iraq," he went on. "It was my third deployment. The third one is supposed to be the charm, but it didn't happen that way. We had big plans. We were in love. But she couldn't handle what happened. I don't have any hard feelings for her. She's a great girl. I still got a soft spot in my heart for her."

"She broke it off?" Jaris asked.

"Yeah, she did," Shadrach replied. "We can't do more than is in us to do. She just couldn't handle it. She couldn't cope with it, not only the injury, but the way I was. I was shattered in my head. I'm an artist. I used to do illustrations for books and magazines. I couldn't even do that anymore."

Shadrach got up from the table and went over into the next room. They all heard a couple of drawers opening and closing. Then Shadrach returned with a handful of illustrations. Some were sketches, and some were watercolors. A few were oils. They were images of people and animals—rabbits and wolves and deer. They were good.

"I made a pretty good living for a while," Shadrach told them. "I'm slowly getting back into illustrations. I live on that, and the government gives me a pension. I'm doing okay. But, you know, it's hard being alone. You lose the ability to really talk."

"Yeah," Chelsea agreed. "I love to talk. I talk all the time. Some of my teachers at Marian Anderson Middle School called me a motormouth."

"I can tell," Shadrach remarked with a smile. "Wow! This is more than I've told anybody in years. You know, Chelsea, you're the one got me going. You're amazing."

The man looked around at the teenagers at the table. "Anyway, I've talked long enough, I guess," he concluded. "Now you know where I'm coming from. I rescued my first opossum, musta been about two, two and a half years ago. I looked into those beady little eyes and I thought, 'Hey, this guy accepts me unconditionally. He just needs a friend. He's not judging me.' I thought that was pretty cool. I didn't think a human being could look at me like that. But then you did, Chelsea."

Chelsea felt so proud and happy to hear Shadrach say that. Strangely, she hadn't tried to make him feel good about himself. She just didn't really care that he was injured. She liked him right away—and that was that.

Chelsea thought briefly about Ms. Colbert and how Falisha felt about her mother being with Shadrach. Shadrach and Ms. Colbert did have something going. Chelsea thought Falisha could change her mind about that. Anybody could change.

"I'm glad we're coming to the opossum rescue place, Shadrach," Chelsea told him. "I've learned so much in just the coupla times I've come. And Maurice is learning too. Maurice was kind of a tough trouble-maker, but being with the opossums has made him nicer. He won't admit it, but he really likes the opossums. He was so proud of holding Magic like that."

"You mean Maurice is turning into a human being?" Jaris asked, laughing.

"Yeah, but he still calls you my 'lunatic brother,' Jare," Chelsea responded. "But he's much better now that he's working with the opossums. I don't know why, but I think the critters bring out the best in people. Even Athena is changing. She's always kinda self-centered and prissy, but she's getting to like the opossums too."

On their way home, Chelsea was tempted to tell Jaris and Sereeta about the friendship between Shadrach and Ms. Colbert. But Chelsea and her new group of friends had made kind of a pact. They had all promised one other that their secrets would stay with the group. And the friendship between Ms. Colbert and Shadrach was sort of a secret. Falisha had trusted them when she shared her dislike of Shadrach, so Chelsea couldn't tell anybody about that. And Ms. Colbert and Shadrach kissing the night they set Magic free, that was a major secret. That was something Chelsea would not share even with Falisha.

Chelsea had seen sad evidence of what happened when gossip got around Tubman. People like Jasmine used it to hurt Sereeta. If the word got around that Shadrach and Ms. Colbert were more than friends, it could hurt Ms. Colbert. Chelsea really liked the teacher, and she wouldn't do anything to hurt or embarrass her.

That evening, Chelsea called Athena. She told her about finding the dead mother opossum and how they couldn't save the babies. "Shadrach was so sweet and nice. I cried, Athena, but he made me feel better 'cause he said I spared the babies a lot of suffering."

"That's nice about Shadrach," Athena replied.

"Yeah, he's one of the nicest people I ever met," Chelsea agreed.

"They're fighting," Athena reported. She sounded strange, not her usual cocky self.

"Your parents?" Chelsea asked.

"Yeah, they're fighting like cats and dogs," Athena said. "It makes me sick. I'm wondering what's gonna happen, you know. Not that it makes any difference, but, you know, I hate change."

"Don't worry about it, Athena," Chelsea consoled. "My parents fight too. Mom and Pop go at it sometimes, but then they make up. It'll be okay. The other night Pop was so mad he drove off in a huff. But then he came back home, and they were all lovey-dovey."

"It's not like that here," Athena responded. "They don't . . . make up anymore."

Chelsea felt a coldness come over her heart. Nothing ever seemed able to upset Athena, but now she was upset. "It'll be okay, Athena," Chelsea assured her. "Tomorrow they'll be better."

"Maybe," Athena murmured. "I gotta go. I'm going down to the twenty-four-seven store and see what's happening there."

"Athena," Chelsea advised nervously, "I wish you didn't go there. It's almost night. I mean, the sun will be going down, and it's, you know, dangerous."

"You should come with me, Chelsea. It's fun," Athena suggested. "I mean, it really is. Guys pass by. And they whistle and holler, and it's fun." Athena was speaking in a wistful voice.

"My parents wouldn't let me," Chelsea replied. "And I'd be scared anyway."

"Okay," Athena said. Then she said good-bye and closed the phone.

Chelsea glanced out the window. The sun had not gone done completely, and the sky still had a lot of red in it.

Chelsea didn't know it, but Maurice had bicycled to the Spain house. He was sitting on the sidewalk, staring at the house.

Jaris happened to notice him. "Chili pepper," Jaris told her, "there's a real creepy-looking punk out there looking at our house. I think he knows somebody in this family. Should I go out there and chase him?"

Chelsea pulled the curtain aside. "Jaris Spain," she scolded him, "don't you dare chase Maurice. He's my friend now. He's scared enough of you."

Then Chelsea realized he was playing a prank on her. Jaris didn't really intend to chase the boy away. Chelsea glared at her brother while he smirked at her.

"Jaris," she told him, "you know how you're always talking about Alonee's posse, your tight little group of friends? Well I got one now too, and Maurice is a member."

"Oh man!" Jaris groaned. "You guys better rethink the membership require- ments for your group if you let Maurice in."

Chelsea gave Jaris a friendly but firm poke as she passed him on her way outside.

"Hi Maurice, wassup?" she asked.

"Is the madman home?" Maurice inquired.

Chelsea giggled. "You mean my brother? Yeah, he's home. But he won't bother us."

"Hey, Chelsea, Heston ain't your boyfriend is he?" Maurice asked her.

Chelsea shrugged. "Pop says I'm too young for a boyfriend, but we hang sometimes."

"He never kissed you or anything, right?" Maurice persisted.

"I don't kiss and tell," Chelsea answered. "But when I was in seventh grade, a boy named LeRoi kissed me in the basketball court."

"Didja like it?" Maurice asked.

"No, LeRoi was a terrible kisser. He almost bit me!" Chelsea laughed.

"I'm a good kisser," Maurice told her. "I'm gonna be the next boy who kisses you, and you'll like it."

Chelsea looked at Maurice. He had deep, dark eyes. He had a wild look when he smiled. He laughed then, and he didn't look so sinister. Chelsea got goose bumps.

"Well, we'll just see about that," Chelsea responded. She couldn't help smiling.

"Maurice," she went on, "me and you and Heston and Athena and them are good friends, right? We got each other's backs, right?"

"Sure," Maurice agreed.

"Maurice," Chelsea continued, "Athena feels bad 'cause her parents are fighting. She's gonna go down to the twenty-four-seven store tonight and wave at guys. I'm scared for her. Could you sorta bike down there and keep an eye on her?"

"You got it, babe," Maurice agreed. "I'll see she's okay."

"I gotta go in now," Chelsea told him. "Pop's making curried pork and sweet potatoes. Thanks, Maurice. I feel better about Athena now."

Chelsea ran inside. Leaning against the closed door, she hugged herself. A strange sense of excitement filled all her senses. She was suddenly so ready to be a freshman at Tubman.

Then something clicked in Chelsea's mind. Shadrach rescued animals. In a way, he saved kids by tutoring them. Jaris was a rescuer too. He had yanked her out of that party where there were drugs and liquor. Now she and her friends were rescuers. Chelsea had even tried to save the baby opossums. Tonight, maybe Maurice would have to rescue Athena from getting into trouble.

"We're all rescuers," Chelsea said to herself. "We're all here to help one another."

She was pleased with that thought. She grinned as she went to wash up for dinner.